Tales of Suspense & Intrigue!

CT Liotta

ROT GUT PUP

Rot Gut Pulp: An Imprint of St. Ire & Sons Publishing, Honolulu, HI

Tales of Suspense and Intrigue!: The Ian Raculmuto Short Stories
from Rot Gut Pulp
Copyright © 2018-2024 by CT Liotta

Library of Congress Control Number: 2024901108
ISBN: 978-1-955394-07-9
Cover Illustration by Zamid Krill
Typography by Corliss Wilborne

Rot Gut Pulp. *Entertainment, Not Genius.* ™

24 25 26 27 28 GN/DN 10 9 8 7 6 5 4 3 2 1/a

First Edition

For Minda, who has encouraged nonsense like this
for over 30 years.

Contents

Relic of the Damned!

When boredom gripped Ian Racalmuto, he made things disappear. At age 7, he started with playing cards and coins, learned from a book of magic tricks. By age 14, he found himself bored so often, he could make any object smaller than a smartphone vanish into the ether.

"Make the dirty dishes in the sink disappear," his Mother would say, "before you begin your Vegas residency."

"We should be a mother-son duo, Deena," he would reply. "You could show the audience how you make vodka disappear." He enjoyed calling his mother by her first name because it irritated her.

Deena huffed. "*Stai zitto, figliolo.* You'd rather me obsess over wine?"

Ian raised an eyebrow. "Lay off my hobby."

"What fourteen-year-old dreams of becoming a sommelier?" she asked. "It's unnatural. Where did I go wrong as a mother?"

"When you paired braised beef with Stolichnaya instead of a cool-climate Tempranillo," he replied.

Deena pursed her lips in thought, and at last flapped her hands. "Your nose isn't big enough to be a sommelier. Play video games with the other kids."

Their argument was irrelevant. They lived in Algeria, where alcohol was difficult to buy. Deena worked for the State Department as a U.S. diplomat. Her husband, Cardiff, volunteered as a dentist for a local charity. Against every imaginable warning, their family had moved from Naples to Algiers—a danger post where the State Department could not guarantee their security.

From the day he was born, Ian had followed his mom to cities around the world. As a result, he had a pan-European accent nobody could trace to a single location. He hated it, but attempts to flatten it made it worse. That he talked with his hands like his Italian relatives frustrated him even more.

Ian's brother Erik, ten years older at 24, had followed Deena into the foreign service and worked in public diplomacy. He was a fan of espionage history, novels, and movies. He waited for the CIA to knock on his office door and recruit him, but they knew better and never did. In the interim, he trained Ian as his agent, teaching him everything he knew about Cold War-era spycraft.

At noon on Tuesday, the brothers drank sweet green tea with mint in a cafe in the *kasbah*—Algiers's lawless residential neighborhood of winding streets inhabited since the second century.

Iron balconies hung above sidewalks in front of louvered antique doors. Laundry, towels, and signs in Arabic stretched over walkways on taut lines anchored to satellite dishes and air conditioner compressors. Graffiti covered ancient brick where plaster had worn away.

Ian, whose soft features and short stature gave other kids the mistaken notion he was a pushover, was taking a day off school following a dustup with a classmate that left him with a black eye. Erik, dressed in a tuxedo shirt with suspenders and a bowtie, was preparing for an event at the embassy when he heard Ian was alone in the *kasbah* and raced to find him.

"You can't come to the *kasbah* alone, Ian," said Erik. "It's dangerous. You're a high-value target because of mom and me. Al Qaeda in the Islamic Maghreb would love to get their hands on you. Al Murabitun's active in these quarters, Daesh-affiliates—it's no joke."

"My schoolmate Kintu lives here," said Ian. "We play soccer in the street and drink Ifri Soda. I didn't get to hang out with him at school today, so I came over."

"That kid's weird," said Erik. "He's around day and night. Do you ever think he likes you a little *too* much? Besides, you *hate* soccer."

"There are other kids, too," Ian shrugged. "All I'm saying is, I keep a low profile. There are about twelve different routes to his house, and I never use the same one twice in a row."

"You're a western teenage boy in the *kasbah*. There is no such thing as a low profile. Nobody is looking out for you. The locals have no clue who you are, and you know nobody here."

A man walked past the café, pushing Ifri Soda bottles on a handcart, and peered inside.

"Ian!" said the man. "*Naharak sa'eed!*"

"People say Algiers is exciting. They say the kasbah is exciting. It's all legend and romance. Nothing happens here except street soccer and laundry."

"Hey Farid!" Ian waved. *"Salamo Alayka!"*

The man ran inside and gave Ian a bottle of cola, then waved goodbye.

"That's Farid," Ian said to Erik.

Erik rolled his eyes.

"What would you have me do?" asked Ian, waving his hands. "It's not like I love Algiers. I'm in a holding pattern and have to eke out some sort of life."

"Find a hobby."

"You know my hobby."

"Wine is not a hobby."

"I enjoyed studying it with dad in Italy, but I'm already losing my nose. I'll not be a famous wine steward unless this country relaxes its rules in the next few months. Algeria is brimming with superb wine, but all for export."

"Your nose isn't big enough to be a sommelier," said Erik.

Ian sighed. "People say Algiers is exciting. They say the *kasbah* is exciting. It's all legend and romance. *Nothing* happens here except street soccer and laundry."

"Maybe you need boredom for a while," said Erik, pointing to the bruise under Ian's eye. He smirked. "Was it over a girl?"

Ian shied away. "It's nothing."

"It was over a girl." Erik grinned. "You'll get taller. Once you hit puberty, you'll grow and they'll like you back."

"Shut up, Erik." Said Ian. "Puberty has come and gone. I'll always be short. I don't mind it. People underestimate me." He caught his reflection in a small flower vase and ran his fingers through his black hair. "The situation was under control and I stayed calm—black eye or not."

"Better to be calm in a situation that's *out* of control," said Erik.

"I'm always calm." Ian lifted his mug and dribbled tea. "Shit!" he screamed, leaping to his feet and flailing.

Customers stared and returned to their food.

The cafe door opened, and a thin black woman in a red dress entered. She crowned her head with a floppy sunhat.

Ian dabbed at his shirt with a thin cocktail napkin. "Anyway, I don't need lectures about situational awareness and girls."

The woman in the red dress drew near. Ian and Erik stared. Her vacant eyes focused a thousand yards past them.

She fell forward onto Ian. The brim of her sunhat smashed against his brow and turned upward. Her lips moved to his ear.

"Berlin," she whispered. She thrust a circular piece of metal into his hands. It looked like a small horseshoe with flattened ends. Her throat gurgled.

"Oh, no," said Ian, collapsing under her weight. "Move her."

The gurgling became more pronounced as she convulsed.

"Erik! *Move* her!"

She vomited blood over Ian's neck and shoulder and fell to the floor, dead. A Douk-Douk El Baraka knife protruded from her back.

"Jesus!" shouted Ian, dripping on the floor. "I told you to move her! Didn't you hear the death rattle?"

"I'm dressed for an important dinner," Erik replied. "You're wearing a second-hand tee shirt. Take one for the team." He pointed to the tiny napkin Ian had been using and flicked his finger. "You were complaining of boredom? *Hai voluto la bicicletta? Allora, pedala!*"

The body settled on the floor. Ian cleaned himself.

Erik examined the metal hoop. "It can't be a bangle or bracelet," he said. "It's too small to wear. And why Berlin?"

"The patina is real," said Ian. "It isn't a replica antique."

Erik said, "An antiquities dealer at a *souk* here in the *kasbah*—Fatimah Farah—has come to the attention of my department at the embassy. A horrible human being. Traffics conflict diamonds. We don't get along. I hate to engage her, but if there's something special about your bracelet, she would know." He surveyed the body, lifeless on the ground, then continued, "We should go. If we're caught with a dead body in the *kasbah* it will cause an international incident."

Tires squealed outside. Erik jumped while Ian scrubbed at his shirt. Three men, their faces obscured by stockings worn over their heads, gathered the cadaver and stuffed it in their car. A fourth sprayed a gentle mist from a small bottle at blood that had stained the floor. In seconds, the blood faded.

The man with the bottle faced Ian and cocked his head. "Ian?" he said. "*Salamo alayka!*"

Ian snatched the spray bottle and misted the stains on his shirt before handing it back. "*Shukran,*" he said in thanks.

Ten years ago, Fatimah Farah had inherited her market shop from her father. She now used it as a front for her crimes. Engineers renovated the building outside, and debris ran from a chute on the roof to a dumpster on the street.

Before entering, Erik and Ian decided that, if separated, they would meet at Ketchaoua Mosque, using *Palais des Rais*, Bastion 23 as a fallback.

"Do you have 200 dinars?" asked Ian.

"No," said Erik.

Ian handed him the money. "Put it in your shoe."

"Why?" asked Erik.

Ian didn't answer. Erik did as his brother instructed, and they went inside.

Farah was restoring a Faberge Egg.

"Hello," said Erik. "My name is—"

"I know who you are," interrupted Farah without looking up. "American embassy officials are not welcome here."

"I'm the one with business," said Ian. "I need an appraisal."

She asked for 2,500 dinars. Ian negotiated, and they settled on 1,000.

Farah stank of camphor from an analgesic patch she wore for lumbago. She gritted her teeth as she bent forward to inspect the hoop. She weighed it, measured it, held it to the light, then let it fall on the countertop and assessed the quality of the sound it made. She made a phone call, spoke in brisk Arabic, and returned to them.

"This hoop is a manilla. It's a form of currency manufactured in Europe but used in West Africa from the 15th to the early 20th century. It is 5.72 centimeters across and weighs 85 grams."

"Brass?" asked Erik.

"Bronze," replied Farrah. "Stolen from Nigeria."

"What's its value?" asked Ian

"A single manilla? Not much. Perhaps fifty U.S. dollars to a collector on an internet auction site."

She placed it under a microscope. Her phone chirped, and she excused herself through a curtain leading to a small back room with an ascending staircase. Silence filled the shop.

Erik examined the ring under the microscope. "Why kill someone over a $50 bronze ring?" he asked.

"Death always accompanies stolen goods," Ian said. "They called copper *the red gold of Africa*. Melted with five or ten-percent tin, it becomes shinier, more durable and more desirable."

Erik scanned the room. "Where did she go?"

They moved toward the curtain. Farah intercepted them with a French military pistol.

"Hand over the manilla," she said.

Ian freed it from the microscope.

"Slowly!" She leveled the gun.

"How did you know someone stole it from Nigeria?" asked Erik, his hands above his shoulders.

"Because *I* stole it," said Farrah, "along with two hundred others. This morning, our count was off by one. Someone in our ranks wanted to get a message to U.S. officials about our activities. She learned your brother was playing football with children in the *kasbah* and found him there."

Erik turned to Ian. "See?"

"Kintu's my friend!" said Ian.

Tires squealed to a halt across the street outside. A man wearing a yellow *djellaba* jumped from the passenger side of a sedan, drew a Caracal pistol, and ran toward the shop. The driver stood, lit a cigarette in a holder, and shouted after him in Arabic. He was a white man with a gray porkpie hat, wearing small round glasses and a trench coat. A strap around his chest held a Tommy gun snug against his back.

Two more men arrived on motorcycles, drew guns, and hurried toward the man in yellow.

Ian palmed the bronze ring with his pinky, grabbed the Faberge egg from the countertop with his remaining fingers, and threw it to the sky. Farrah gasped and moved to catch the egg, pinched a nerve in her back, and screamed. Her gun clattered on the floor. Ian and Erik sailed past her, through the curtain, and up the stairs.

Lanky Africans filled a room at the top of the staircase on the second floor. They gripped diamonds with tweezers and scrutinized them through small telescopes attached to their glasses. Ian and Erik burst through the doorway, ran to the middle of the room, and spotted two men sorting through a wooden crate filled with manillas. The men startled, slapped a loose wooden lid down on the crate and ran with it to the door.

"Go!" shouted Erik, following them.

The men with the crate disappeared into the stairwell, replaced by the man in yellow and his lieutenants. Ian and Erik halted, turned, and fled. Gunshots cracked. Bullets whizzed past. They scrambled through a window and up a fire ladder.

"No shooting!" Farah's disembodied voice sounded from the first floor. "The diamonds! *Tu détruiras tout*! Idiots!"

Ian was first to the roof and pulled Erik to the top. On the ground below, the Africans with the manillas strapped their crate to the back of a motorcycle and took off through the streets. The man with the porkpie hat let off a half dozen rounds from his Tommy gun. Smoke from the weapon mingled with a wisp streaming from his cigarette. The bullets struck at Ian's feet.

"Did you see that?" asked Ian. "He's shooting at us with a 1921 trench broom—forward grip and all. I think the Kerr strap is original, too. Mom has nothing like it in her collection."

Erik pulled him back. "Follow the motorcycle!" he said.

The brothers sprinted to the corner of the roof. The motorcycle turned onto a cross street. They followed it from above, colliding with hanging clothes on laundry lines and old women beating carpets draped over balustrades. The man in yellow climbed onto the roof and fired his handgun in bursts, sending the bystanders scattering. An elderly woman fell over dead, shot in the gut.

Erik led the way to a shed—a stairwell outlet. The gunman's accomplices exited from it and took aim. "The debris chute!"

Ian gathered a shingle remover at his feet and dove for the oversized funnel on the roofline. Bullets sank into a barrel of roofing tar next to him. When he landed in the dumpster below, the man with the gray hat greeted him with the business end of his Tommy gun.

"The relic," he said. "Hand it to—"

Ian swung the shingle remover into his face. The man recoiled. Ian ran for the second motorcycle beside the sedan and took off in pursuit of the manillas, rounds from the Tommy gun chasing him.

On the roof, Erik occupied the two gunmen who had emerged from the shed in a maze of hanging clothes. Mistaking one another for him, they shot each other dead through a bedsheet.

The man in yellow fired his weapon and sprinted for Erik as Erik followed Ian, below. A round grazed Erik's bicep.

In front of them, a ten-foot chasm stretched between buildings.

Erik surmised he could escape, if he could jump, but power lines stretched between him and the ledge beyond.

He dove forward, anyway. Solid ground dropped from under him. He cleared the power lines by inches and reached for the edge of the building, catching it and struggling over the top.

The man in yellow, too, dove from the rooftop toward Erik. His foot struck a power line, redirecting him into dozens of others. A magnificent flash of light exploded as his flesh sizzled from his bones. When there was nothing left, his charred, smoking skeleton crashed to the street below.

———

Erik Racalmuto did not see Ian at Ketchaoua Mosque as planned. It was prayer time, and busy. He moved on to Bastion 23, the *Palais des Rais*.

The *Palais des Rais* was a historical lot in the lower *kasbah* comprising three palaces and six houses dating to 1576. An example of Ottoman architecture with horseshoe arches, magnificent tile, and carved Arabesques, it reminded Erik of a Las Vegas hotel where his mother threw dice.

A short brown man collected admission. "200 Dinars," he said. Erik turned over the money in his shoe. It was damp with sweat. The man scoffed in disgust.

The *Palais* was empty. Erik's shoes echoed. On a terrace on the second floor, he found Ian sitting atop an old cannon that pointed to the Mediterranean Sea. He had the top of the wooden crate in his hand.

"How'd you find your way here?" Ian asked.

"I jumped rooftop to rooftop," replied Erik. "Shadows are pointing east-southeast at this time of day, and I oriented myself toward the mosque. I eventually heard the call to prayer as *Asr* drew near and followed the sound. When I didn't see you at the mosque, I came here. How did *you* find *your* way here?"

"I stole a motorcycle," said Ian. "It's downstairs."

"Give me the keys," said Erik. "I need to find a dry cleaner before tonight." He looked at the lid Ian held. "You lost the manillas?"

"I got something better."

He pulled an enormous diamond from his pocket, stolen from Farah's counting house, and displayed the wooden lid. Somebody had marked the top *Mineralogic Specimens* and addressed it to Director Helmina Weizenbaum of the *Museum für Naturkunde* in Berlin.

"The dead woman said *Berlin*," said Ian. "What are we doing the rest of the week?"

Erik sighed. "We're not going to Berlin."

"Please?" Ian beamed. "The museum has a dinosaur hall. I like dinosaur bones and stories of the extinction event."

"*You're* going to have an extinction event," Erik murmured.

———

At 4:40 the following morning, Ian and Erik sat on a Boeing 737 at Boumediene airport. It taxied to the runway.

"This is a terrible idea," said Erik. "What if mom finds out?"

"We'll be home by dinner," said Ian.

After a transfer at El Prat the Racalmutos arrived in Berlin at 10:30. They made some phone calls, got lost on the U Bahn, and arrived at the *Museum für*

Naturkunde as it closed for a special event. Erik convinced the staff they had important business.

Beside a three-story high sauropod skeleton in the main atrium, Ian inquired for Director Weizenbaum of the mineral collection. He assessed the skeleton while he waited and said, "this is a *Giraffatitan*. A sauropod. The tallest dinosaur skeleton in the world. 13 meters high."

"I get it," said Erik. "Like a giraffe, with a long neck. What's beside it?"

"*Diplodocus*. A replica of the one in Pittsburgh," replied Ian. "Go Bucs." He pumped a fist.

A docent approached with a message: Director Helmina Weizenbaum would meet them by a meteorite in a wing devoted to the solar system.

Ian and Erik climbed hard marble stairs to the second floor. In a dim rotunda, a seven foot-long thousand-pound meteorite swung overhead on rope from the arm of a crane. A black woman in her mid-twenties stood under it and made notes.

"It's rare to see the underside of this meteorite," she said. "The museum is updating the display stand."

Erik read a placard. "This came from Africa?"

"Kinshasa," said the woman. "I wish the museum would return it."

"No," said Erik. "If curators moved this to the Democratic Republic of the Congo, nobody would ever see it. Travel to the DRC is nearly impossible. Plus, museum guards would chip away at it to sell pieces to collectors. Nothing would remain of it to see."

The woman's mouth went flat. "It belongs to the people of Kinshasa. Its presence here justifies imperialism, and your perceptions of museum guards there are prejudiced if not racist."

Erik said, "My point is, nobody *goes* to Kinshasa. Cultural relics placed in major world cities encourage international exchange and give more people access."

"Which further privileges Western scholars and European academics," the woman interrupted. "Cultural property is part of my job. Don't dare lecture me on it."

"Repatriating cultural artifacts is part of *my* job," said Erik. "Don't lecture *me* on it."

"Are you Frau Weizenbaum?" Ian interrupted.

The woman glared at Erik. "I'm her intern, Alexandra Njenga." She turned and extended her hand to Ian. "Frau Weizenbaum is taking hallucinogenic pills in the staff lounge."

"Ian Racalmuto," said Ian, taking her hand. "This is my brother, Erik. Hallucinogenic pills?"

"Frau Weizenbaum is brilliant but suffers from chronic *Lebensmüdigkeit*. The pills allow her to overcome the dismals and leave bed in the morning. She hires interns for tasks that require functionality. I'm from the University of Abuja, Nigeria."

"Our great-grandmother was from Lagos," said Ian.

"Then your brother should know better than he does," Alexandra smiled. "You have no African features. You were adopted?"

"We're seven-eighths Italian," said Erik. "Our grandfather looks like her."

"Grandpop tells me I have great-grandma's shrewd brains," said Ian.

"At least one of you does," said Alexandra.

Shoes echoed on the floor.

"Ms. Weizenbaum," said Alexandra, becoming serious as a well-dressed woman in a pantsuit appeared. "Erik and Ian Racalmuto. They are here because," she paused, "we didn't get that far. Why are you here?"

Ian removed the manilla from his pocket and unwrapped a handkerchief he had been using to protect it. "This is yours?" he asked.

Weizenbaum positioned it before her nose. Her vacant eyes grew wide. She grinned. She lowered the relic and stared at Ian in silence, her smile glowing on.

"Erik?" said Ian from the side of his mouth. "Do Germans normally grin like this?"

Erik stood behind Ian, looked over his shoulder, and waved a hand in front of Weizenbaum.

Weizenbaum's head tilted to the side, and she emitted a shrill cackle.

"A dead woman gave it to me in Algiers," Ian continued. Could she hear him, or did his voice echo as though shouted into a tin can? He spoke slower and louder, like he might to a senior citizen. "The dead woman whispered 'Berlin' before she vomited blood all over me."

Erik plucked the manilla from Weizenbaum and thrust it to her face. "We put the pieces together. You're receiving a shipment of stolen artifacts. Count them, and you'll find this one's missing. The jig is up. What I want to know is why these are important. Why is someone trying to kill us over a worthless hoop?"

"Worthless?" Alexandra interrupted. "Do you know what you're holding?"

Erik turned to her. "It's a Nigerian bracelet worth about $50 on eBay."

"It's a manilla," she corrected. "Europeans manu-factured them as currency to trade for West African slaves." She ripped it from his hands. "This is blood money!" She spat on the floor. "You have no right to possess this, or to deem it worthless!"

He snatched it back.

Weizenbaum swatted at the air as if driving away flies, took the manilla from them, and dropped it in her pocket. "I'll return."

She said nothing more and left, floating on an invisible tide.

"How dare you," Alexandra continued to Erik. "Fifteen manillas for a slave. Fifteen for women and girls like your great-grandmother, sold in the markets of Calabar."

"How dare me?" He thrust his thumb at his chest. "I'm not the one who ordered a stolen crate of them! People are trying to kill me. I don't have time to get bent out of shape about the stupid, morally bankrupt culture of a bullshit trading society that operated three hundred years ago, five thousand miles away."

Alexandra's eyes widened. "Intelligent groups of people lived along the Cross River," she said. "I'd appreciate you not judging and belittling their beliefs using modern contexts and frames."

"And I'd appreciate *you* acknowledging that people died over bullshit ideas and beliefs," shouted Erik.

"Why don't you explain it to me, like I haven't lived in Nigeria my entire life?" said Alexandra.

Weizenbaum returned, wobbling in a stupor. Ian held a silencing hand. The director's pace quickened. She drew close. Then she threw herself on Ian and gurgled. An El Baraka knife protruded from her back.

"Not again," said Ian. He struggled to hold her upright. "Erik!"

She vomited blood over his shirt and collapsed to the floor. He threw her down, only to see the Englishman with the gray fedora rounding the corner. A bandage covered the wound where Ian had struck him with the shingle remover.

Three brutish men stood at his side. Two brandished pistols.

"*Ahlan*," said the man. His accent was British. "Or should I say *Guten Tag*?" He drew a Luger P08.

Alexandra backed toward the crane.

"Is that a Luger?" asked Ian. "You have an impressive eye for classic weapons."

"Hand me the relic," said the man.

Erik went through Weizenbaum's pockets. Next to a bottle of pills, he found the manilla.

"Inform our superior the collection is again complete, and that Frau Weizenbaum has... outlived her usefulness." He held the hoop and became lost in the shimmering bronze. "Kill them."

"Timo!" Jarvis shouted to his remaining button-man, "Kill them!"

The two henchmen with the guns stepped forward into the center of the atrium.

Alexandra pressed a button on the crane and the suspended meteorite crushed them from above. A pistol discharged.

Jarvis startled and dropped the manilla. It rolled to Ian's feet. Ian gathered it and ran, Erik and Alexandra close behind.

"Timo!" Jarvis shouted to his remaining button-man, "Kill them!"

Timo Bendel, a rough man with clothes like a stevedore, did not carry a gun. He had no fingers to pull a trigger. Instead, he killed with a razor-sharp titanium boomerang that he pinched between his nubs and threw with tremendous biceps.

The brothers and Alexandra ran through a mineral exhibition room with antique display cases. Bendel's boomerang sliced through three cabinets. Rock samples and glass shards covered the floor. Ian handed the manilla off to Erik and ducked before the boomerang could remove his head on its return.

Bendel caught the boomerang by clapping his palms together. Had he known to catch the boomerang by clapping when he first used it, he would still have his fingers.

Jarvis fired his Luger at Erik, destroying fossils in a specimen cabinet. Erik threw the manilla to Alexandra.

Alexandra entered a room containing wet specimens - 276,000 glass jars on shelves with a million animal samples floating in preservatives. Bendel's boomerang missed her by inches before tearing through a collection of lampreys and fetal beasts. The weapon landed on the floor and Bendel bent to collect it.

"I can't predict its flight path," Erik shouted.

They moved to the dinosaur hall. Jarvis fired his Luger again, this time missing Alexandra and striking the *Diplodocus*. The beast's hind leg spun across the room and the skeleton crumbled. Guy wires suspended the mess of bone from the ceiling like a twisted art installation.

Bendel heaved his boomerang at Erik. It tore through suspension wires supporting the skeleton of the *Giraffatitan* and lodged high in the creature's thigh.

Alexandra tossed the manilla to Ian through the dinosaur's rib cage. Ian caught it and lifted the *Diplodocus* leg from the floor.

Bendel climbed the sauropod skeleton to retrieve his boomerang. He squeezed his legs around bone to stabilize himself, clasped his weapon between his nubs, and rocked to free it. Ian swung the *Diplodocus* bone into the *Giraffatitan's* ankle. The towering skeleton collapsed sideways. Bones rained onto the marble floor. The air crackled. Bendel fell sideways and screamed. A rib impaled his lungs, and he became still.

Police sirens wailed outside. *Bereitschaftspolizei* stormed into the dinosaur hall, now an unrecognizable pile of dust and bone. They arrested Ian, Erik and Alexandra. The man with the porkpie hat had disappeared.

Polizeihauptmeister Günter Heiner paced back and forth in the Racalmuto's hotel room and clenched his square jaw. Ian and Erik sat on a bed in front of him. Deena and Cardiff, having arrived from Algiers, sat at a table nearby. Doctors had encased Erik's wrist in a plaster cast. The *Giraffatitan's* skull had crushed it as it collapsed to the floor.

"The manilla?" asked Heiner.

"Alexandra threw it to me," said Ian, "but I have no clue where it landed. It's likely under the pile of bones in the museum."

The *Polizeihauptmeister* grunted. "We searched and found nothing. Your story would be unbelievable even if we had the object."

"Forgive me, Herr *Polizeihauptmeister*," said Erik. "If we had the manilla, how do we know to trust *you*?"

"You must trust *somebody*," he replied. His subordinates had searched Ian and Erik and found only the bottle of hallucinogenic pills Erik had taken from Weizenbaum.

"You were high?" asked Heiner, inspecting it.

"The pills belonged to *Museumsdirektor* Weizenbaum," said Erik.

"They're illegal," said Heiner.

"I believe it," said Ian. "She was completely off her tits. You need to find a man with a trench coat and a porkpie hat."

"He is German?"

"English," said Ian. "He has an accent. Geordie, I think."

Erik added, "His colleagues were German. In Algeria, they were Algerian. He hires locals."

Heiner scribbled notes. "Damage estimates are close to a billion dollars. Dinosaurs. Mineralogic specimens. Wet specimens. Priceless."

"Don't forget the giant meteorite Alexandra dropped from the crane," said Ian.

"Yeah," said Erik. "Send *her* the bill for that one."

"Surely we can come to an agreement," Deena interrupted from the corner. "I'm a consular with the State Department. Erik is a diplomat as well."

"Are you traveling on diplomatic passports?" asked Heiner.

"No."

"Then you are tourists," said Heiner. "Fortunate for your government. Contact your embassy in Berlin and secure legal counsel. I will make notes downstairs. Do not leave this hotel." At that, he left.

No sooner had the door closed than Deena Racalmuto shouted, "*A Tommy gun?*"

Ian scrambled up the bed to the headboard.

"Do you know how long I've wanted one? How could you not take it from him?"

"I had no time," said Ian.

She paused. "Where did you find the money to buy plane tickets to Berlin?"

"I used a conflict diamond I stole from a thief," said Ian.

Cardiff remained calm. "Ian, you're grounded. Erik, you know better than to get involved in situations like this. You're teaching your brother bad habits."

Deena pointed at Ian and screamed in Italian. "You should be in school." She then switched her gaze to Erik. "And you! You requested time off and boarded an international flight hours later? Did you not think that diplomatic security would notify *me* and pursue *you*?"

"The DSS couldn't care less about my whereabouts," said Erik. "I'm a low-ranking public diplomacy officer. They don't know where I am."

There was a knock at the door. A diplomatic security officer entered and introduced himself. He had questions for Erik. Deena raised an eyebrow.

"I give up," said Erik.

Ian paced as Erik left the room. He approached Deena. "There's an indoor pool off the corridor near the lobby. Did you bring my swimsuit?"

"You're grounded," said Cardiff, looking up from a book.

"Go to the lobby," said Deena. "Bring me a finger of Kleiner Feigling from the bar. Neat. When you get back, we'll talk about the fight you got into a few days ago at school."

"Can I get a glass of wine? They have Leitz pinot noir."

"You're grounded," repeated Cardiff.

———

Interior designers had constructed the hotel lobby with bright white Calacatta marble. They used a special forklift to place an enormous reception desk along the wall. The floors were white. The walls were white. White lights illuminated white artwork and white statues. A bar opened to both the lobby and a restaurant on the other side. Ian, in no hurry to order his mother's vodka, sat in a white armchair and played with a white matchbook. He made it disappear and reappear. Two girls with long brown hair watched him from a distance while their parents talked to the bell captain.

A stack of luggage clattered as it fell. An African boy with a kind face, twisted hair, and an aloha shirt had tripped on it as he wandered in from the street. Sweating and out of breath, he surveyed the room.

The concierge intercepted him. "This is not a public lobby," he said.

The boy turned. "I'm looking for him," he said, nodding toward Ian.

The concierge brought him to Ian. "You know him?"

The African boy cocked his head and smirked. The mannerism made Ian smile. He looked at the boy, then at the concierge. "We're old friends," said Ian. When the man had left, Ian said to the boy, "you look like somebody I know, but with better hair. Alexandra's brother?"

"Ashura," said the boy, shaking hands and smiling. "Alexandra sent me because I'm inconspicuous."

"You're doing a fantastic job," Ian laughed.

Ashura spotted the girls with the brown hair. "Beautiful women at this hotel. They haven't taken their eyes from you," he said.

"It's annoying," said Ian. "They're fawning at me like a puppy. I can't be bothered with them right now. It's been a terrible day."

"I heard as much," he said. "It's why I'm here. Alexandra is in trouble."

Over five minutes, Ashura did not break eye contact as he explained his situation to Ian. He was fifteen. Alexandra was raising him. He left Nigeria after having difficulties at school and now lived with her in a studio apartment. School in Berlin was better. He knew German and worked a maintenance job to help with expenses.

With the museum in tatters, Alexandra's internship—and their visa status—had become uncertain.

"If we overstay our visas, we'll have to hide." Ashura looked down at himself. "I'd be no good at it."

"Not in that shirt," said Ian.

Ashura cocked his head and smirked again. "If you can find the missing manilla and prove what happened and who did it, it will exonerate Alexandra of guilt and secure her position with the museum. We'll be able to stay. She won't have the same opportunities in Nairobi she does in Berlin." He stood to leave. "Alexandra will stop by later today. I can't stay."

"Why not?" asked Ian.

"I have a date tonight with girl I've liked since last year." Ashura took a step to the door. "It was good meeting you, Ian."

"Wait," said Ian, putting his hands in his pockets. "Do you like magic?"

Ashura stopped.

"Give me a Euro coin," said Ian.

Ashura handed one over.

Ian continued, "I have a way to go to prove what happened and who did it. However—" He passed the coin over his knuckles and into his palm. When he turned his hand around and opened his fingers, in place of the coin was the manilla.

Ashura snickered. "Why haven't you shown it to anybody?"

"I don't yet know who to trust," said Ian.

"Hand me the relic," said a close voice in a familiar British accent.

Ian didn't bother looking up. "You've got to be kidding me," he mumbled, handing Ashura his Euro coin. "Run."

As they moved, a lanky woman with blond hair and large white sunglasses stopped them with a small derringer.

"This derringer killed Lincoln," she said. "It will not pause for you."

Ashura dropped his coin. It rolled under a chair. The woman led them along a corridor and down a staircase.

They arrived in a garage used for deliveries, closed to the public. Inside was a military-style Leyland service truck with enormous tires. A canvas roof covered the lorry's flatbed.

"Start the motor, Jarvis," the woman commanded.

The man with the trench coat sealed himself in the cab and cranked the ignition. The engine roared, and diesel fumes belched into the room.

The woman motioned the boys into a corner of the garage, where they sat on overturned buckets. She handcuffed them together to a worktable.

"My name is Vinita Clapp," said the woman, removing her sunglasses. She then removed her hair and placed it in a plastic bag. "Do not mind my appearance. *Alopecia totalis* is benign, if shocking. As a young girl, I took steroid injections to the scalp." She placed a ball cap with an attached ponytail on her bald, white head. "My doctor did not give lollipops. As for the matter at hand, you do not understand the damage you have caused. Hand over the manilla."

"I no longer have it," said Ian.

"I will ask you one last time." She withdrew a rusty pipe cutter from a drawer. "Then, I will remove fingers."

"I can still throw a boomerang," Ian said.

Clapp was unamused. "In that case, I will remove your friend's fingers."

Ashura swallowed hard.

Ian handed over the relic. "What's this about, Clapp?"

"I am forty-five years old. I see old age as clearly as youth. I'm taking vapors at night and my doctor tells me that the climacteric is near."

Both boys shifted. Ashura rubbed his temples with his free hand.

She continued, "I am an archæologist by trade." Ian could hear the ash. "As I decline, I wish to surround myself with pleasing objects. Rare objects. Some, I discover. Others I steal. Let other people have fast cars and cash. I want stones from the Pyramids of Giza. Ceremonial pipes from the Iroquois. Porcelain from the Goreyo Dynasty. I can buy gems at the Mall. There is only one musket that killed President Garfield—and one complete collection of manillas directly linked to Captain Thomas Phillips of the slaver *Hannibal* prior to its infamous voyage of 1694.

"The truck in front of us contains a decade of accumulated treasures. I am moving them across Europe to Casablanca where I am constructing a lair for their display."

The garage now stank of fumes.

"And the classic weapons you and your people carry?" asked Ian.

"Part of my collection," she said.

"Building an eccentric collection as you reach your climacteric can't be your only motivation," said Ian.

"A complete manilla collection with direct links to the transatlantic slave trade is a priceless museum piece. I can insure it for twice the value of the Hope Diamond. $500 million American dollars." Her eyes watered.

"That makes its black-market collateral value even more substantial," said Ian.

Clapp smiled and coughed. Black smoke hung in the air. "And now, gentlemen, Jarvis and I must leave for coffee while the truck exhaust suffocates you. Good morning." Jarvis exited the cab, buckling and gagging. Clapp threw the keys to the handcuffs over her shoulder. They slid under the truck, out of reach.

Diesel fumes filled the garage. Ian and Ashura choked, and their heads swam. With their free hands, they searched for tools that might pry apart the handcuffs that locked them to the table. They discovered nothing.

Ashura closed his eyes and settled back. "What a waste. I'm going to die before I can go on my date."

"What's her name?" asked Ian.

"Mila." He coughed and grinned. "Big-boob Mila. She was with another guy until last month. I finally got my shot. Do you have a girlfriend? You seem the type."

Ian shook his head in the negative and wheezed. "I live in Algeria. I have no options. Too many cultural barriers."

"None of that matters," replied Ashura. "When you fall in love, nothing stands in your way. You want to follow that person to the ends of the earth. Nasty parents, society rules, different cultures, dangerous neighborhoods—it all drops away. You do anything to be with them."

Ashura's voice became distant as Ian's thoughts drifted to the streets of the *kasbah*. Blue sky. His lack of skill playing soccer. Bottled soda in the hot sun. The room blurred. Objects turned to shadows.

As he slipped from consciousness, the corridor door opened.

Alexandra Njenga mashed a button on a control box and opened the garage door. Air rushed in. She covered her nose with her shirt, grabbed a monkey wrench from the wall, shattered the lorry's side window, and stopped the motor. Under the truck, she found the keys to the handcuffs.

Ian's head bobbled.

"We were looking for you," Alexandra said to Ian, unlocking the boys. "Erik saw the man from the museum with a woman with the manilla in the lobby. She put the relic in her *décolleté*."

"Her what?" asked Ashura.

"Her big boobs," said Ian. "Does *Polizeihauptmeister* Heiner know?"

"Without a doubt. The man from the museum recognized Erik and opened fire. The police responded. When I left, both the woman and the police were calling for reinforcements. I don't know what's happened since."

An explosion outside rattled the hotel.

Ian and Ashura, still recovering from headaches, ran upstairs with Alexandra. Deena and Erik met them in the corridor.

"How did you find them?" asked Erik.

"The concierge was watching my brother on a security feed," said Alexandra. "I saw the woman throw her keys under the lorry. Where's your father?"

"Upstairs, asleep. Jarvis has a half-dozen gunmen looking for us."

"*Goons*," said Alexandra. "*Gunmen* is gendered language."

"They're men," said Erik.

"You're perpetuating sexism," said Alexandra.

"Can I say nothing right?" asked Erik

"You haven't, yet."

"Go easy on me, will you? My wrist is broken. The cast itches."

"Don't center the conversation on your pain."

"Christ's bloody cross," muttered Erik.

Distant gunfire and screaming issued from the lobby.

Deena turned toward the noise. "I never got my Kleiner Feigling," she said. She pointed her finger in Ian's face. "I'm putting a stop to this. *Dovresti essere a scuola*. You're missing class. Erik and I need to be at work. Both of you have worried your father sick. He's to perform a root canal tomorrow, and his hands are shaking."

"But, mom," said Ian.

"Don't *but mom* me," she snapped. "Algeria is ravaged by dental caries, and he's taken the vapors."

"I have to take a leak," said Erik. "I'm going to find a toilet." He looked at Alexandra. "A *men's* room."

"Don't get your cast wet," said Alexandra.

In the lobby, *Polizeihauptmeister* Heiner shot at Jarvis, who fired his Luger from behind an overturned divan. Heiner's deputies and Jarvis's associates shot from every angle, and bullets bounced from the white marble. Guests at the hotel covered their heads and screamed.

One of Jarvis's men, a lanky Dresdener, positioned himself behind a statue of Nero bathing. He fired a Walther P38 with one hand and carried a second in a sloppy holster on his hip. A bottle of Henkell Brut chilled in a bucket on a nearby cafe table.

Deena rounded the corner, lifted the bottle and smashed it into the man's skull. She took his guns, and with one in each hand laid waste to three of Jarvis's men as she walked at a resolute pace toward the bar.

Jarvis stood from behind his divan. His Tommy gun swung from the strap across his shoulder. He pulled the firing bolt.

Deena dove behind the front desk. Jarvis fired two hundred rounds in a single burst before his gun jammed. The rounds bounced wall-to-wall, floor-to ceiling. A porter, several police officers, three tourists, and two of Jarvis's own men fell dead. A lifeless slug landed next to Deena.

Blood streamed from Jarvis's ears, which rang from the noise.

Deena poked her head above the desk. Jarvis stared at her for a beat, jiggled the firing bolt, and waddled through the lobby into the corridor. She and Heiner crossed the room in chase, certain the two of them would have no problem catching the awkward man with the heavy gun as he made efforts to free a stuck round.

Jarvis entered through a door marked *Schwimmbad* and locked the door behind him.

Heiner called for a tactical ram and minutes later, they were through.

In a humid room, Jarvis stood near a set of locker room doors at the deep end of an indoor swimming pool. He had fixed his machine gun and fired ten rounds into the pool to prove as much. Plumes of water rose into the air.

Heiner extended a hand. "No sudden moves," he said.

"I will kill you, with or without sudden moves," said Jarvis. "Before I do, I want the lady to know I will kill her children before the day is out."

Deena's eyes narrowed.

Someone tapped Jarvis's shoulder. He turned, and Erik Racalmuto, who had been in the locker room urinating, struck him in the jaw with his plaster cast. Jarvis had not heard him approach because of the ringing in his ears.

The cast exploded in a plume of dust that covered Jarvis's face. His glasses flew to the floor, and he teetered at the lip of the pool.

Erik gripped the strap on the man's Tommy gun and forced it back. Jarvis tumbled into the water, thrashing as the heavy gun dragged him below.

Deena screamed.

Heiner would not recover Jarvis's weighted body from the bottom until workers drained the pool later that day.

"Goddammit, Erik!" said Deena as the bubbles stopped and the silhouette underwater became still. "You ruined the Thompson!"

The hotel lobby was silent. People collected themselves as police took command. From behind the bar, Deena poured deep shots of vodka for anybody who wanted one. Alexandra and Ashura waited. Ian scanned the floor. Spent cartridges. Broken glass. Purses, earrings, spectacles—and a ball cap with a ponytail connected to it.

Where was the bald woman? Ian caught sight of her white dome. She climbed alone into a basement-bound elevator. He ran to the stairwell, his friends close behind.

They beat Clapp to the garage.

Ian pulled the keys from the ignition of the Leyland truck. "Hide!" he instructed.

"You don't know how to fight this woman," said Alexandra.

"I have it under control, said Ian.

Ashura concealed himself in the truck bed and Alexandra hid behind a fuel drum. Clapp entered the room.

Ian met Clapp in the middle of the room and held her keys to his ear. "It's over, lady," he said.

Clapp sucker-punched Ian in the stomach. He crumpled to the floor, and she took the keys.

Alexandra sprang from hiding and beat the woman like a schoolyard bruiser.

Clapp screamed and shielded herself. She could not reach the derringer strapped to her thigh.

Ribs. Kidneys. Nose. Everything crunched under Alexandra's knuckles. She dropped the keys and collected them again. She was not sure how she made it into the truck. Blood streamed from her nostrils. Ashura remained in the back, and Ian jumped in beside him as Clapp pulled away.

The tremendous lorry sped past the Brandenburg Gate along the *Straße des 17. Juni*, neither stopping for lights nor slowing for traffic. Its right fender struck a pedestrian and plowed into a U-turning car. Clapp stomped the gas.

The police gave chase.

The tremendous lorry sped past the Brandenburg Gate, neither stopping for lights nor slowing for traffic.

Ian scrutinized the flatbed. "We're about to become part of Clapp's collection," he said.

"Why not be the *only* thing in it?" asked Ashura. He threw a box of Spanish coins out the back.

Piece-by-piece, Ian and Ashura emptied the truck of its cargo. Statues. *Objets d'art* packed in straw. Jewelry.

"You may still make your date tonight," Ian said.

"I'll jump out of this truck if I have to," said Ashura.

Sirens blared behind them.

"Hey Ashura?" asked Ian. "Strange time for a question, but how did you know Mila liked you? How do you know when *anyone* likes you?"

"Why do questions of love preoccupy you?" asked Ashura. He wagged a finger. "You have somebody in mind back home."

Ian grew silent, and Ashura grinned.

They turned a box of World War II-era rifles onto the street.

A helicopter flew low overhead, and the truck slowed.

"Police?" asked Ian. Officers in a patrol car behind them looked up. Several drew guns and shot skyward. The truck bounced as it decelerated and rolled off the paved road. Ashura and Ian stumbled forward as the cab crashed into the Victory Column in Tiergarten. They exited unhurt.

A rope ladder fell from the chopper into a row of surrounding trees and flew away. Clapp had vanished.

Ian and Ashura had finished with *Polizeihauptmeister* Heiner when Alexandra and Erik arrived in a taxi. The door opened. The two screamed at one another, this time over whether Erik's idea of opening a Mexican restaurant in Algiers constituted the cultural appropriation of food. Erik shouted last words about *mole poblano* as Alexandra ran to Ashura. Erik found Ian.

The boys were talking. Ashura was mid-thought. "It's easy to tell if a girl likes you. They show up where you do. They don't complain about you being around too much, even if you are. They remember everything you say, like it's written in the Bible in red letters. The telltale sign, however, is if her friends and family suddenly know everything about you. It means she speaks of you night and day."

"That could describe most of my friends in Algiers," said Ian. "I fascinate people because I'm foreign and hang out in the *kasbah*. They all talk about me. Girls *and* guys."

"What I speak of is different," said Ashura. "When boys are around each other, they aren't smitten and foolish as I'm describing. If they are, they're wrong in the head. It wouldn't be normal."

"Yeah," said Ian, shoving his hands in his pockets.

"Dating advice?" Erik interrupted. "I can tell you all you need to know."

Alexandra burst into laughter. "Jesus wept," she said.

Erik turned away. "Mom and dad are on their way," he said to Ian. "Mom keeps making the cab driver stop so she can pick up the antique guns you threw from the van. Dad keeps making him stop to pick up relics he wants to return to indigenous tribes."

"You could learn a lot from your father," Alexandra said to Erik. "You should be more like him."

"I'm not a bad guy," said Erik. "If you buy me a drink tonight, I'll prove it—even if I failed to retrieve your little brass hoop."

Alexandra shook her head and produced the manilla from her pocket. "I did not need your help. It slipped from the vile woman's bosom when she bent down to gather her keys." She checked the time on her phone. "I have to clean up the museum. *You* have to clean up your attitude. I'll see you again. Irritating people hang over me like an umbrageous cloud."

A tow truck struggled to haul the wrecked Leyland away.

"I have to go home in the morning," Ian said to Ashura. "I can't go swimming. They're draining the hotel pool to remove a body."

Ashura's phone buzzed with a text. "Mila!" he said. "She wants to meet early."

Ian shrugged. "Anyway, If you're ever in Algiers, look me up."

"Sure," replied Ashura, now lost in his messages. "Give me a shout if you're back in Berlin." He glanced up. "I only have an hour to get ready."

He scrambled toward his sister, and together they hired the taxi Erik and Alexandra used earlier. Ian waved as they sped away. Alexandra caught his eye and waved back.

———

Erik and Ian sat on opposite ends of a white sofa in the hotel lobby. Stuffing protruded from bullet holes.

"I won't lie," Erik sighed. "I like Alexandra. I would have helped her put the museum back together if she asked. Maybe I'll get to fight with her again, some-day."

"I was hoping to hang out with Ashura tonight," said Ian. "It didn't materialize, either. He had a date."

"I overheard," said Erik. "It's not quite the same, *fratellino*. You'll understand when you find a girl you like." He stared out the window and paused for a beat. "Can I say something to you without it being awkward?"

"Can I say something to *you* without it being awk-ward?" Ian replied.

"Go," said Erik.

"Sometimes, when people tell you you're wrong, you are," said Ian.

"Sometimes, when people tell you you're wrong, you aren't," Erik replied. "Continue."

"We all have blind spots," said Ian. "I'm not saying Alexandra was right about everything, but maybe you'd make some headway with her if you took a little time to digest what she was saying instead of being so defensive and sure of how the world works."

Erik nodded. "Yeah."

"Now, what are your thoughts?" asked Ian.

"People you like can have a limited concept of what's normal and what's—" he gripped Ian's scalp and messed his hair, "wrong in the head."

Ian ducked and fought him off.

Erik continued. "Not everybody who thinks they have life experience and good advice really has. You'll know someone likes you when they'd rather spend an extra hour kicking a ball around the *kasbah* with you than texting other people on their phone."

Ian flicked his eyebrows and stared at the floor.

"Too on the nose?" asked Erik.

"Shut up," Ian replied.

Erik held out a fist. Ian looked over and pounded it with his. He smiled at last.

Beside the brothers, a concierge lifted an overturned chair upright. Ashura's Euro coin was beneath it. Ian picked it up.

After a moment, Erik said, "You never told me what your fight in school was about."

"No," said Ian, making the coin disappear. "I didn't."

END

DEATH IN THE CITY OF DREAMS

At one minute past noon on a hot, overcast day in Mumbai, a bomb exploded at the *Chhatrapati Shivaji Maharaj Vastu Sangrahalaya* - the city's museum of antiquities. Visitors screamed and ran out the doors, hair white with plaster dust. One man, close to the blast, evaporated into a pink mist.

Only an hour earlier, 14-year-old Ian Racalmuto sat in the back seat of a taxi between his mother, Deena, and his grandfather, Mario. "Can we skip the Chhatrapati Shivaji Maharaj Vastu Sangrahalaya today?" he asked. "It's hot, and I don't feel like going to a museum." The car had no air conditioner, and Ian's black hair dripped sweat that ran over his soft face. His father, Cardiff, sat beside the driver. They bantered in Hindi and English as hot wind blew through an open window.

Mario touched a handkerchief to his brow. The old black man spoke in a fluent mix of English and Italian. "*Sono d'accordo*," he said. "Ian's right. You collected me moments ago from Chhatrapati Shivaji International Airport. The museum may be too much Chhatrapati Shivaji for one day." He leaned toward Cardiff. "When you and Deena left Bombay a decade ago, I never dreamed I'd return. It's no vacation destination. There's been a spate of bombings. This city is hot, crowded and dangerous."

"*Che cavolo*, dad!" said Cardiff as he looked over his shoulder. "Why did you join us if you don't want to be here?"

"Philly's boring. It's a slow month for commissions at the store."

Deena said, "Ian was only four when the State Department moved us from Mumbai. He didn't get to experience it like the rest of us."

"Why does Erik get to stay back at the hotel?" asked Ian.

"He's exhausted," said Deena. "Plus, he suffered through my tour of the Chhatrapati Shivaji Maharaj Museum ten years ago, when *he* was your age. Now, it's your turn."

"Why do I have to suffer through it twice?" asked Mario.

"It takes persistence to get things through your skull," said Deena. "If we were to do an MRI of your head, it would show a tiny, cultureless brain filled only with thoughts of undermining my parental authority."

Mario checked the time on his phone, half-ignoring her. "And boobs," he added.

Ian cackled. So did the driver, who looked at Mario in the rearview mirror and wagged a finger.

"He's fourteen, Mario!" shrieked Deena. "He hasn't even had a girlfriend!"

"Relax, Deena," said Ian. "I'm not a child."

"Don't call me Deena!" said Deena. "And YOU!" she reached over and stabbed her finger in Mario's face. "You know better!"

The driver turned to Cardiff, grinning. "He is your father? Why is he dark, like from Africa?"

Mario sat forward. "My father was from Sicily. My mother was from Kenya. I *am* African, by half."

Cardiff added, "My mom was Italian. That's why I look less like dad."

The driver looked back at Ian. "You look like a westerner, only," he struggled for the word and looked at Cardiff, "*chhota*?"

"Short," said Cardiff. "Most westerners are tall."

"I like being short," said Ian. "People underestimate me."

"He has his mother's looks, but don't let it deceive you," said Mario. "He has his great-grandmother Racalmuto's brains."

"Ian's oddity is his accent," said Deena, rubbing the back of Ian's hair. "He flails his hands when he talks like his father, but nobody knows where he learned his patois when he speaks English."

"I don't mind being short, but I hate my accent," said Ian.

"You sound more ridiculous trying to hide it," said Mario. "People act ridiculous when they try to hide things. That's how you know they're hiding something. Speaking of that, can I have my pocket knife back?"

"What knife?" asked Ian.

Mario raised an eyebrow.

Ian slumped. He withdrew Mario's knife from his pocket and handed it back. He had a talent for sleight-of-hand and picking pockets. His grandfather was the only person able to detect his machinations.

———

"Perhaps instead of the museum we can go to the tower of silence on Malabar Hill," said Mario.

"That's not an attraction for tourists," said Cardiff.

"What is it?" asked Ian.

Mario leaned toward Ian. "It's a squat, wide, round tower where they excarnate the dead!"

"It's part of the Zoroastrian faith," said Deena. "Only people who practice Zoroastrianism may use it, and only a chosen few caretakers venture inside. When Zoroastrians die, the caretakers put their bodies inside the tower of silence, in one of three concentric rings."

Mario interrupted, "Then buzzards fly down and pick the corpses clean! It called a sky burial. The bones bleach in the sun before the caretakers push them into a central pit where they disintegrate!"

"I want to see *that*!" said Ian.

Cardiff flailed his hands. "It's a solemn site, not an object for your amusement! Deena, tell your father-in-law to knock it off."

"I need a martini," she said, biting a finger.

After time in traffic, the taxi arrived at the Chhatrapati Shivaji Maharaj Vastu Sangrahalaya. The family got out of the cab and stood at a distance. The enormous onion-domed Indo-Saracenic building, Deena explained, was not Indian but a British imitation of Indian design. As she pointed out elements stolen from the Taj Mahal, the front of the building turned to dust and blew toward them. A second later, hot wind and the sound of an exploding bomb knocked them to the ground.

Police cordoned off the entrance and questioned the Racalmutos. Sand caked their clothing. An officer and the cab driver screamed at one another in Hindi. Deena and Cardiff walked over to intervene.

"I guess the museum's closed," said Ian.

Mario stared at the front door, then at the side of the building. "Your mom wanted you to see the museum. Let's fulfill her wishes."

They walked to a side wing. They shared the same gait - a slight waddle that belonged to Mario's father generations ago. A docent with thick black eyebrows and shiny shoes pointed discombobulated people to exit doors. He stopped Mario and Ian from going inside. Ian did not hesitate and pleaded with the man. "My sister is inside! I have to find her!"

"I guess the museum's closed," said Ian.

Mario watched Ian beg and cajole. After a minute he produced 300 rupees and put it in the man's shirt pocket. The man bobbled his head and looked away. Ian and Mario entered.

"Did you see his shoes?" asked Mario as they walked into a gallery.

"They were shiny," said Ian.

"They were perfect," said Mario. "As were his trousers. A man who cannot afford shoes trades in good deeds and mercy as currency. A man with perfect shoes is greedy for a second pair. When there's urgency, ask kind favors of those with nothing, and pay those who have everything. That's how you grease the wheels."

"Did you learn that in the CIA, Grandpop?" Ian had long suspected that, in a different life, Mario was a spy.

The old man gave a sideways glance. "Spies don't exist. I work in men's clothing at Wanamakers."

The museum was empty. Fire alarms no longer sounded, but emergency strobes continued to flash. The sound of shattering glass drew Ian and Mario to a room at the end of a short passageway. They arrived as a fat, bald European man wearing a pointed white sidecap closed a round tiffin lunchbox called a *dabba*. It looked like a long steel coffee can, but with three nested layers held together with clips. He carried three more on a strap around his shoulder.

He looked up, saw Ian and Mario looking at him, and ran. Ian gave chase. The big man breathed through his mouth and limped. Mario watched them go around the corner.

Another bomb exploded.

———

"I almost had him," said Ian. His hair stood on end and black soot covered his face. Blood ran from one nostril.

"Goddamit, Mario!" screamed Deena. "Look at him!"

"I'm fine, Deena," said Ian. "I hid behind a sandstone Sadashiva relief when I saw the man throw a tiffin can toward me."

"Don't call me Deena!" screamed Deena. She turned to Mario. "Do not teach him how to play this game, Mario."

"I won't," said Mario. "I'll teach him how to win this game."

Deena's face reddened. As she opened her mouth to argue, a black sedan approached. The driver, Police Inspector Ranjit Bharucha, lowered his window. "Hello, Deena," he said.

Her anger dissolved. "*He* can call me Deena," she said, giving him an awkward hug through the opening. Bharucha blushed.

"Some things for you," he said, handing her a .32 caliber IOF break-action revolver and a bottle of White Mischief vodka. "Only the essentials."

She looked at the gun and smiled. "I've wanted this gun for my collection for years. Thank you. How are you?"

"I'm losing sleep over a rowdy-sheeter blowing up my city. Rest is fine." He stepped out of his car and introduced himself to Ian. "I used to work with your mother at the embassy, when she was starting her career as a diplomat. When I last saw you, you were three or four. Erik followed your mom into a career with the State Department?"

"It's turning into the family business," said Ian.

"Is that your plan, as well?"

"I want to be a sommelier—a professional wine advisor."

"Your nose isn't big enough." Bharucha withdrew a notepad. "So, you met our bomber?"

"You're looking for a squat fellow, about 1.7 meters tall," said Ian. "He wears a white hat that looks like an upside-down boat—the kind that they wear at candy and ice cream shops. Also, he was carrying a load of round metal lunchboxes."

Bharucha laughed. "You've just described 5,000 men in Mumbai. *Dabbawalas*. They're a well-orchestrated profession that carries lunch tins to businesspeople throughout the city every day. The white hat is called a *Ghandi cap*."

"This guy is white, fat, bald, carries explosive lunchboxes, and wheezes when he walks. He limps with a bad right hip. That should narrow it down."

A constable shouted from the museum and waved at Bharucha. He held a Ghandi cap in one hand and a four-layer round tin lunchbox in the other. "Inspector! We found these inside a gallery!" he said.

Bharucha's eyes widened. "Put it down and get away!" he screamed.

"What?" cried the man, raising the dabba above his head.

"Put it down and get away!" Ian, Mario, and Deena shouted and waved in unison.

A bomb team arrived a half hour later and cleared the lawn where the man had dropped the tin. They inspected it using a radio-controlled robot with fiber-optic cameras. The top layer contained half-eaten *naan*. The bottom three layers were inseparable and housed a secret chamber. Inside, the bald man had packed the can not with explosives, but with a priceless Mahavira statue from the display case.

———

On the ride home, Deena turned to Ian. "Because the museum didn't work out, you can come with me while I buy shoes."

"You're kidding me!" said Ian. "Please, no!"

"No backsass," she said. "There's a shoe store in the Taj Mahal Palace Hotel. I deserve new shoes after today. Then, you can pour me two fingers of vodka and visit with your brother."

"I can't go to a museum without shit happening," said Ian. From under his shirt, he produced the lid from the bomber's lunch pail. It was marked in a series of letters, numbers, and colors. He handed it to Mario. "I pinched this from the crime scene. Dabbawalas use these markings for delivery. I cannot read them, but maybe they're a clue. Erik used to date a girl from Mumbai. Aadarsha Betawadkar. She'll know what it means or know people who do."

Mario bristled. "Erik hasn't talked to Aadarsha since university. She hates him."

"Her parents don't."

———

It rained late in the afternoon, slowing travel in Mumbai. Ian and Erik arrived later than expected at an upper middle-class apartment block. Aadarsha Betawadkar's mother, overjoyed to see Erik after many years, welcomed the brothers into her home and made pakora and chai. Aadarsha locked herself in her bedroom and refused to come out.

"This is no way for a grown woman to act," said her mother, rapping at her door. Aadarsha gave no reply.

When Ian produced the lid to the bomber's lunch can, Aadarsha's father, Ashok, took *his* lunch can from the kitchen to compare markings. He was too proud to wear bifocals and lifted his distance-vision glasses to his brow to read.

"Dabbawalas paint a simple shipping label on the lid. On the right, vertical, is the destination address." He pointed. "This is my office address. The number in the middle represents the train station nearest my office. Surrounding it are two bits of information. The wala who collects my tiffin must go to a collection point, indicated by one marking. At the collection point, other dabbawalas take it to an origin train station. That is the second marking. It is complex, but dabbawalas seldom make delivery errors."

Ian sat back. "So, you hire somebody to carry your lunchbox to work every day through a circuitous network of collection points and train stations? No offense, but why can't you carry it yourself?"

"I leave at six AM. My wife would have to wake at four to make my lunch. It would be cold. Nobody likes cold tiffin."

His wife laughed. "There is no room on the commuter train for people to carry dabbas. The trains are very crowded. Riding requires both hands for balance. Dabbawalas can make use of the baggage cars. Our *wala* comes at 10 AM. His people deliver at the office promptly, at one."

"Everybody in the city of Mumbai uses this service?"

"Not everybody, but over two *lakhs*."

"Two *what*?"

The man smiled. "Nearly a quarter-million people send their lunch to work through dabbawalas every day."

Ian stared at the lid. "The origin station is written in *Devanagari*, and I can't read it."
The man lifted his glasses again. "Grant Road."

A door opened. Aadarsha Betawadkar appeared from her room. She wore a bright pink kurta that covered a pair of Levis jeans. Black hair came to her shoulders. She said hello to her mother and spoke about household matters in Hindi. Erik stood. She approached him and backhanded him so hard, he spun. His lower lip bled.

"You rotten bastard," she said. "I told you never to speak to me again."

"Hello, Aadarsha," said Erik, feeling his lip. He looked at Ian. "Never break a girl's heart."

"That wasn't for breaking my heart. That was for killing my chinchilla." She slapped him again, forehand, in the head. "That's for breaking my heart."

"You killed her chinchilla?" asked Ian.

"I forgot to feed it when she left university for two weeks to come home."

"You didn't forget," said Adarsha. "You never listened in the first place."

"It's in a better place," said Erik.

She backhanded him again. "The neighbours called the police because of the smell, Erik! When I returned, Akshay had turned to liquid and bone. I took the blame! The foreign girl with the rotting pet in the apartment! Do you know how that feels? Do you care? Now, here you are. In my living room. Cozying up to my parents. Talking to them with your silver tongue, I'm sure, and making me look like an unreasonable bitch. Did you bring gifts?"

Erik reached into a bag, "I have tea for your mother. It's her favorite variety."

The old woman grinned and blushed and reached out to receive the gift. Aadarsha knocked it from his hands and onto the floor. "Get out," she said. "When I passed out of university, the only consolation I had was that I would never see you again. Don't you dare utter another word."

"I need you for an adventure," said Erik.

She cracked him across the face again. "Goddammit, Erik!" she said. "I told you not to say another thing!"

There was silence.

"Where?" she asked.

The following morning, Ian, Erik, and Aadarsha took a motorized three-wheel auto rickshaw - a *tuk-tuk* - to the Grant Road suburban railway station. There, a busy dabbawala looked at Ian's lid and pointed Aadarsha to a collection point in Kamathipura before rushing off. There, dabbawalas wearing white Ghandi caps brought tiffin cans from surrounding houses and apartments and prepared them for rail transit to their final destinations.

Nobody bothered to talk to the visitors. At last, a 13-year-old girl approached. She waddled her head as she spoke to Aadarsha. Aadarsha told her to go away.

"She thinks she's a dabbawala," laughed Aadarsha.

"I speak English," said the girl. "And I *am* a *dabbawali*."

"Do any of the dabbawalas know?" asked Aadarsha.

"Do you want help or not? I'm busy."

"What's your name?" asked Ian.

"Do you want help or not? I'm busy."

"Mita Gavande," said the girl. "Your good name, please?"

"Ian Racalmuto. This is Erik and his ex-girlfriend, Aadarsha." He showed her the lid. "Where did this come from?"

She took the lid and asked around. When she returned she said, "Come."

Mita led them to a small restaurant. Three tuk-tuks sat outside. Inside, there were no customers and no tables. Stacks of empty tiffin cans formed round towers in a corner. The tile floor in front of a worn counter was dirty with footprints. An old woman behind the counter prepared lunch for delivery. When she found a moment to break, she talked to Ian. Aadarsha translated.

Ian produced the lid and explained how he found it.

"Auntie says her restaurant is delivery only," said Aadarsha as the old woman spoke and became tearful. "Somebody has been taking her tiffin cans over the past month. She works hard to earn fifteen hundred rupees a week and replacing them cuts into her bottom line. She does not deserve this. She fasts and prays and honors the gods."

"Fifteen hundred rupees?" asked Ian.

"About twenty-five bucks," said Erik.

Ian's shoe had come undone, and he knelt to tie it. When he did, he noticed tubular rubber shavings on the floor. He picked one up as he stood, then looked at the ceiling. "Are you having electrical work done, Auntie? It looks like somebody is shaving wire around here."

Erik looked at the stack of dabbas, then at the old woman. Her tears ceased as fast as they had come on, and she ran to the back of her store. As she did, the bald museum bomber appeared. On a strap over his shoulder was a collection of tiffin cans.

The fat man recognized Ian. He ran forward, pushed the boy into the stack of empty tiffin cans, and limped out the door as they crashed down. Aadarsha watched as he pulled away on a tuk-tuk.

Mita helped Ian up. "Are you going to let him get away? Get on a tuk-tuk!"

"I can't drive a tuk-tuk," he said.

"I'm not asking you to!" she replied.

———

Mita and Ian got into one of the tuk-tuks, while Aadarsha and Erik got in the other. The women drove fast in pursuit of the bald man, sounding the horn and sending children and salespeople scattering as Ian and Erik held on.

"How did you become a dabbawala, Mita?" asked Ian.

She concentrated on the road. "It's *dabbawali*. I'm a girl. My uncle is a tiffin wala. I used to follow him on his route. Are you familiar with Mahim Creek?"

"No."

"It's a fetid waterway used by people in the slums for toileting. Last year, for two days, it became clear and turned sweet. It remained unsafe, but thousands of people called it a miracle and drank, even as garbage floated past. My uncle got gastroenteritis. While he was in hospital, I took over his duties. I am now developing my own client list."

She broke hard to avoid a manhole and sped up again as they kept pace with the bomber.

"How's business?" asked Ian

"Up 100% since last month. I now have two cus-tomers. I need one *lakh* rupees to get my business started. Where will I come up with it?"

"I'm still not clear what a *lakh* is."

"A hundred thousand. About $1,500 US dollars. I want to set up a computer routing and tracking system. Do you work?"

"I'm a student," said Ian. "My brother loves spycraft and taught me the trade, but I want to be a professional wine advisor."

"Your brother is a spy?"

"He's a diplomat. He should have been a spy. He's lousy at diplomacy."

She twisted the throttle on the tuk-tuk and again laid on the horn.

Behind them, Aadarsha twisted her throttle to keep pace.

"So, Erik? How are things with Mayra?" she asked. "Married yet?"

"It didn't work out."

"You cheated?"

"She didn't like me. Why do you think I cheated? I never cheated on *you*."

She rolled her eyes. "That's a matter of opinion."

He sighed. "It would be a lie to say I don't miss you, Aadarsha. People think I'm an asshole. You know I am for certain. You never tried to fix me. Instead, you accepted it. Only, you left."

"Why try to fix somebody else's nature? People can only fix themselves. You should fix yourself. The gods can upend your life at their pleasure."

"The gods have failed every time they've tried."

"If they can't get to you, don't be surprised when they destroy the world around you."

They sped through Chor Bazaar, a section of the city overflowing with knick knacks and gold chains, replica antiquities, and counterfeit watches. The bomber threw a dabba toward Ian and Mita.

"Brace yourself!" screamed Ian.

The metal tin rolled into a shop peddling second-hand luggage. An explosion sent scraps of fabric and leather against Ian and Mita's tuk-tuk as its right wheel lifted from the ground. Erik and Aadarsha sped past, through the rising heat.

The bomber sped on and threw another tin behind him. The blast killed a woman selling old radios on the sidewalk and knocked the support beams from a balcony. Soot blackened the air as the balcony crashed down, tearing the façade from a store that sold antique tea kettles, musical instruments, discarded road signs and bike tires.

"Brace yourself!" screamed Ian.

The bomber turned right onto Mohammed Ali Road, past Minara Masjid under the JJ Highway flyover. Giant concrete T-columns elevated a four-lane highway over kebab stalls, merchants and jammed local traffic. The bomber drove his tuk-tuk onto the sidewalk. Crowds of screaming people jumped from its path. He struck a woman holding a baby and did not slow.

Another tiffin can sailed toward Ian and Mita. It struck their windshield, bounced off, landed under a T-column, and exploded. When it did, the four-lane highway above them buckled and collapsed. Ian and Mita remained in pursuit of the bomber. Erik and Aadarsha disappeared into the rubble.

Mita slowed.

"Keep going!" shouted Ian. "Don't let him go!" He continued looking back through the dust, hoping to see signs of his brother.

The bomber stopped in front of an Italianate Gothic revival train station that consumed two city blocks.

"Victoria Station?" asked Ian.

"That name vanished years ago. It is now the Chhatrapati Shivaji Maharaj Terminus." said Mita.

"I've had enough Chhatrapati Shivaji Maharaj for this trip," said Ian. "He has brought me nothing but trouble."

The bomber again favored his right hip as he entered the station. Ian and Mita followed. For a few seconds the madman disappeared in the throng of people beneath the Victorian clocks and domed Gothic ceiling.

Ian spied him through an archway, entering an office marked *accounting*. Mita pushed through in pursuit.

The accounting office was busy with laborers, confused about Ian, Mita, and the limping, wheezing man who had passed through moments before. A 1,000-kilogram metal door slammed shut and clinked as the bomber turned a lock from inside.

"Where does it go?" asked Ian.

A flurry of Hindi passed between Mita and the ticket office workers. "An abandoned room in the basement once served as the station treasury. Nobody has used it in decades. This door has always sealed the room.

Everyone presumed the keys lost. Lately there has been activity. Their supervisor forbids them from discussing it.

Ian studied the door and found a keyhole. Mita found a second, hidden among decorative embellishments. "It is a security door. It requires two keys," she said.

Across the room a dumbwaiter connected to a pulley on the ceiling. It passed through a two-foot hole in the floor. There was barely enough room in the gated elevator to hold a strongbox. An accountant talked to Mita.

"The lift is unused but operational. Accountants once used it to transport coins between this office and the treasury chamber. It would take the strength of three men to operate the pulley and drop it into the basement, with the weight of the coins. The railway no longer uses coins as it once did."

"Have you seen anything going down the elevator recently?" asked Ian.

"Yes," said the man. "Tiffin dabbas."

An older man with glossy shoes and a white mustache approached. He wore a name badge that read *R. Kadeem*. When he learned that Ian and Mita were asking about the door to the basement, he removed them from the office. As they left, he placed four loose keys in a teacup on the corner of his desk.

When Erik Racalmuto regained a sense of awareness, he was on his back looking up at five old merchants who had removed him from the wreckage of his tuk-tuk. One had been chanting "*Aum Namo Narayana*" into his ear. Content to see his eyes open, the merchants scattered to help other people.

The air stank of oil and smoke. Cars from the flyover had crashed down onto the road below when the support column gave out. Traffic had stopped. Bystanders carried the deceased to the middle of the road as distant emergency vehicles approached.

Erik lifted his head. His tuk-tuk was on its side. He limped over. Aadarsha was still in the front seat.

"Once more the gods have failed," he said. "Do you think we can turn this upright?"

When she did not answer, he noticed the blood on her head. The five old merchants rushed over, freed her from the wreckage, and carried her to the row of bodies.

"Wait!" said Erik, as they laid her out. He ran over and slapped her face. "Aadarsha?" Her pulse was weak.

The men hurried away and returned with a cadaver.

"We can't just leave her here in the road!" he screamed. By then, they were removing pieces of concrete to free other people.

He slapped Aadarsha's face again, tore his shirt to bandage a wound, and elevated her feet. Sweat soaked his clothing. His lips were gray with concrete dust, and his mouth was dry. Unable to speak Hindi, he found help nowhere. Not far away, another section of the flyover crashed down. Erik covered their noses and shielded them from the debris cloud. He slumped beside Aadarsha, drew her hand to his cheek, and struggled for air as he sobbed.

At last, an ambulance arrived and took her from the heat. The driver would not allow Erik aboard.

———————

The following morning, Mario Racalmuto looked around the abandoned store from which Auntie had run her tiffin service. Ranjit Bharucha, Ian, and Mita followed through the front door. Deena, uncomfortable in a new pair of shoes, shifted back and forth outside as she asked Auntie's neighbors about the old woman.

"I did not know her," said a woman wearing a colorful *shalwar kameez*. "She arrived days after the owner of the restaurant died and never gave her name. I remember only one dabbawala entering and exiting her shop - the white man."

Mita found charred remains of *pav bhaji* on a flat griddle. The burner had gone cold when a cylinder of cooking gas ran out.

"Looks like Auntie split while we were on our tuk-tuk ride," said Ian.

In the back room, stacks of tiffin cans in various states of assembly littered a workbench. Bharucha rubbed his finger along the surface and inspected the residue.

Deena entered the shop and gritted her teeth as she stepped over debris.

Mario removed a plastic box from a satchel. He then swabbed surfaces with gauze and sprayed the gauze with chemicals.

"What's that?" asked Deena.

"It's a bomb detection kit," said Mario.

"Where did you get a bomb detection kit?"

"I stole it from the security checkpoint at the airport. I helped myself while they were busying themselves with a tube of toothpaste in my carry-on. It's a nice kit. I wanted to prepare myself."

"You know better than to carry toothpaste in a carry-on, Grandpop," said Ian.

Mario smiled. "Do I?"

"Jesus take the wheel," said Deena, throwing her hands up toward Mario and turning to Ian. "Ian, you are never to put toothpaste in your carry-on so you can distract airport security and steal their bomb detecting swabs. Do you understand?" She shifted her weight and buckled her knee.

Ian looked at her shoes, and back to her. "Whatever, Blisters."

Mario giggled.

"He only acts this way around you!" said Deena.

"No traces of chlorates, bromates, or black powder," said Mario.

Deena handed Ian a cobalt blue dropper bottle from her purse. "Place two drops of this on your grandfather's gauze."

Ian watched the swab change color.

"RDX and nitro-cellulose," she said. "Likely Semtex."

"Cool!" said Ian. He looked at the dropper bottle. "Where did you get this?"

"I had a half-bottle of Grey Goose in my computer bag until we went through airport security," said Deena.

Mario harrumphed.

Bharucha made notes and asked if he might keep the bomb swabs. He then crowded at the counter with Ian and Mita and discussed the previous day's events. "A heavy metal door leading to an underground treasury? In the accounting office at Victoria Station?"

"You mean the *Chhatrapati Shivaji* Terminus," said Ian. "They changed it."

"He means the *Chhatrapati Shivaji Maharaj* Terminus," said Mita. "They changed it again."

Bharucha made a phone call outside and returned ten minutes later. He bounced a curled knuckle on the countertop. "It is more than an underground strongroom. When Frederick William Stevens built Victoria Station in the late 1800s, his architects included a tunnel that ran between the Terminus and the Reserve Bank of India, a kilometer away. It was both dangerous and impractical to carry money from the station overland. By the end of the 20th century, the RBI stopped taking unsorted money. The accounting office made deposits at closer branches, and the strongroom fell into disuse.

"That there are people using the old room, that one of them may be our mad bomber, and that the room is connected by a corridor to the RBI are troubling details. To get into the room, one must go through a series of two heavy doors that require four keys. Nobody knows where the keys are. By the time our detectives find a way in, it could be too late."

"There's a narrow dumbwaiter," said Mita, "operated by rope-and-pulley. The footprint is two feet square, but the lift is four feet tall. It's meant to haul coffers filled with money, but I bet it can fit a short person."

They both looked at Ian.

"You're short too, Mita!" said Ian.

"I'll be right behind you," said Mita.

Deena approached from the back room. "My feet are killing me. I need to go back to the hotel and check on Erik and Cardiff. What are you three scheming?"

"Nothing," said Ian.

Ranjit Bharucha traveled to CSMT station with Mario, Ian and Amita. Two of Bharucha's deputies met them. In the accounting office, managing agent R. Kadeem became displeased when Bharucha asked to access the cargo lift leading to the basement. When Kadeem tried to block access with his body, Bharucha called his deputies to arrest the man for questioning.

"Do you have the keys to the metal door?" asked Bharucha.

Kadeem's eyes traveled to the teacup on his desk.

"Thank you," said Bharucha.

Kadeem dove across the room, reached into the teacup, and ate two of four keys inside before his coworkers restrained him.

Bharucha peered into the cup and shook the remaining keys, then looked at Kadeem. "Is somebody paying you to keep people from going downstairs, or are you doing it for ideological reasons?"

"Money," said Mario. "Shiny shoes."

"Those will hurt coming out," said Ian.

Bharucha posted two guards by the heavy door, then helped lower Ian into the basement using the lift. As Ian descended from view, Mario said, "Don't die. I can't stand to listen to your mother's nonsense when she's upset."

Ian saluted with two fingers.

———

The lift landed on a concrete floor around the corner from an anteroom. The sound of muted voices echoed. Ian drew closer and listened as the elevator went back up to collect Mita. There were racks of tiffin cans on two wheeled carts in the anteroom. The bomber stood beside them with five laborers. Commanding their attention was a woman wearing a sari. She had long, black hair that touched her waist. She secured a set of door keys in a pocket.

"Gaddis," she said, looking at the bomber, "You're an idiot. I asked you to tag the carts." She had an American accent.

"I did," he said, pointing to small cream-colored paper tags on the corners.

"These men are illiterate, and not even I can read your handwriting."

"Actually, India has a 75% literacy-"

"Shut up!" she shouted. She appended two different tags, one red and one green. "Red goes to the bank. Green goes to the airport."

She paused and wiped her brow. "Is anybody else hot?"

Gaddis said, "My arthritic hip hurts from the bullet wound -"

"I don't care!" She removed her long, black hair to reveal a bald, white scalp. "I paid three thousand dollars for this wig. It is sacred hair from Andhra Pradesh. The cap is supposed to be ventilated, but hell if it is." She waved it in front of her to cool off. "The tops of my feet itch. Why are my feet so hot and itchy?"

Ian spun with his back to the wall to avoid detection as Mita landed and joined him.

"Well?" she asked.

"Clapp!" whispered Ian. "Vinita Clapp! She's an archæologist who tried to kill me in Berlin. She steals relics from museums and holy sites."

"Why is she fanning herself with her wig?"

"She's menopausal and having a crisis at mid-life."

A man beside Clapp spoke on a walkie talkie, then turned to his associate and chattered in Hindi. The group walked down the hallway toward the bank.

Ian and Mita entered the cool stone anteroom. British designers had built a safe into the wall during the colonial period. Mita wiped off a brass plaque that dedicated it to queen Victoria.

Ian opened the tiffin cans on the cart with the green tag. Inside were rare coins, treasures, and antiquities. "These came from the museum," said Ian.

"Not the coins," said Mita. "They are old. If this tunnel leads to the Reserve Bank of India, it's possible that Clapp used it to empty vaults."

Mita opened a tiffin lid on the cart with the red tag. Gaddis had smashed curly wire into plastic explosive.

Ian pulled the red and green tags from the carts. "The green-tagged cart contains treasure. The red-tagged cart is to go under the bank that Clapp robbed-"

"To cover my tracks in a massive ball of fire!" thundered Clapp as she and her men returned. She pointed a derringer at Ian. "Hello, again. I would congratulate you on discovering my scheme, but it's too simple to warrant reward. Please replace the tags and raise your hands."

Ian did.

"Gaddis, take them to the darkroom."

———

The fat, bald bomber led Ian and Mita to a windowless room deep in the tunnel between the train station and the bank. It smelled like mold. A naked lightbulb hung over two wooden chairs, bolted back-to-back. Gaddis yanked Ian's shirt over his head and removed it, then threw it into the hallway. He then tied Ian and Mita to the chairs with thick rope.

Clapp joined them. She held a cricket bat and handed it to Gaddis. He said nothing and swung the flat side into Ian's face. Ian passed out, and Clapp revived him with a bottle of water. "It only gets worse," she said, holding Ian's chin. His face began to swell. "That little tap doesn't begin to pay for the riches you cost me in Berlin."

She nodded to Gaddis. He swung again, this time hard into Ian's side. The boy screamed as a rib broke. Mita could see nothing, but her chair vibrated when the paddle connected, and Ian's scream deafened her.

"Who are you, and why do you follow me around the world? How did you find me?" asked Clapp.

Ian opened his mouth to reply, but Gaddis swung the bat before he could- this time into his upper chest. Ian thought his lungs had collapsed. When he could breathe again, he began to cry.

Gaddis bent down to Ian's face. "Is crying the best you can do? Do you want to go home?" He swung the bat again into Ian's flesh and screamed, "Heroes don't cry!"

Clapp took the bat from Gaddis and turned to Mita. "And you, guttersnipe. Do you have anything to contribute?"

Mita said nothing.

Clapp circled them. "There is nothing in this room, as you may have noticed. No light. No food. Not even a lock on the door. There *is* air, and there are hungry rats that come through the cracks in the walls.

"This afternoon I finish my plans and leave Mumbai. You won't hear us as we fly overhead. Not down here. After that, it is unlikely that anybody will find you before you have turned to bone. If you survive the explosion, you need not worry about food. You'll dehydrate before you starve to death."

She turned to leave, but then spun once more and drove the edge of the bat into Ian's stomach. He passed out, again. She threw the cricket bat into the corner, turned the light out, and closed the door behind her.

When Ian awoke, Mita had been calling his name for twenty minutes.

The room was so dark, Ian wasn't certain his eyes worked. His face felt puffy and hot. "This is a hell of a mess," he said.

"Your grandfather and the police will look for us," said Mita.

"If Clapp has her way, we'll blow up before my grandfather and the police get through the door. I think she broke my ribs."

"You shouldn't listen to the fat man," said Mita, after a few seconds. "Sometimes heroes cry. Despair hurts."

"So does having a cricket bat driven into your head."

"But that's not why you cried. Hopelessness is a fine reason to cry, too."

"But it isn't why."

"Why pretend things differ from what they are?" asked Mita.

"How would you know?"

"Because girls know. Do you have a girlfriend, Ian?"

Ian fidgeted against the ropes. "Yes. Back home."

"Why are you lying?"

"I'm serious."

"What's her name?"

"Su... Susa... Sama..."

"Fuck it," she interrupted. "For being a half-decent spy and a superb confidence man, you're lousy at lying about girls. Do you like girls?"

"*Yes*!" Ian shouted. "What the hell? I'm a *guy*." He struggled against his restraints.

"Wait! Do you hear that?" asked Mita. Ian stopped struggling. They listened in the silence. "That's the sound of my eyes rolling into the back of my head."

"Oh, shut *up*! Being beaten up with a cricket bat was preferable to listening to you!"

"If you like girls, we should go on a date. You're cute and I clean up well. If you don't like girls, don't make up a bunch of stupid lies about having a girlfriend and rules about how life should be. You deprive yourself of personal growth."

"What are you *talking* about? Rules like *what*?"

"I'm a guy! Guys like girls!" She mocked him as she waddled side to side in her chair. "A good secret agent makes a career of assuming a disguise and being dishonest with people. Outside that disguise, he should not be dishonest. Otherwise, he does not know which of his two faces is real. There will be no hope for you as a spy if you cannot live in honesty outside the job."

"You have it all wrong. I don't want to be a spy. I want to be a sommelier."

"Your nose is not big enough." A sharp pain coursed through Mita's big toe. She yelped and kicked her foot. When she did, it connected with a mass of fur that hit the wall in front of her. It squeaked.

"Ian?" she said.

"Let it go, Mita" said Ian. "You're making way too much of nothing. I haven't met a girl I've liked, yet, is all." He felt movement on the chair between them.

Then, he felt claws against his neck. He threw his head forward and something scattered on the floor.

"Ian, how many rats travel together in a pack?"

A creature ran between their feet. Ian felt sharp teeth biting at his leg and kicked.

The sound of scampering on the stone floor became more pronounced. So did the awareness of other life in the room. Creatures crawled across their shoulders and over their heads.

A loud metallic clink reverberated. The door opened. The corridor lights blinded them. Erik Racalmuto held Ian's shirt. "Holy shit! He screamed. Look at the size of those rats!"

"Erik?" yelled Ian, turning away from the light.

"Your shirt was outside the door. You'll need antibiotics. And a rabies shot."

"Get us out of here!"

The light sent the last of the rats back into the walls as Erik untied them. "Grandpa brought me to the station. When we arrived, the accounting office was closed. I picked the lock. Everybody inside was dead, including the guards that Bharucha posted. Murdered. We were worried about you and Mita. The big metal door was open, so I came down. Grandpa went to find Bharucha."

"It's Clapp again," said Ian, putting his shirt on. It hurt against his skin. "If she left the metal door unlocked, she'll soon return."

They ran to the anteroom. Workers had taken the red-tagged dabbas away. The green-tagged rack was still there. They heard voices. Clapp and Gaddis descended the stairs.

"You have the remote detonator?" asked Gaddis.

Clapp replied, "In my handbag. I'll press the button at the airport, prior to departure. Now that the explosives are in place, have our men take the green cart upstairs using the lift. Go to hangar 12 at the airport. You have the concussion grenades?"

"Yes," said Gaddis, opening a vest to reveal them, "but why concussion grenades? And why hangar 12? Our plane is in hangar ten."

"Shah Rukh Khan's airplane is in hangar 12," said Clapp.

"The Bollywood actor?"

"He has a nicer jet. I'm stealing it. Your concussion grenades will see us through any obstacles. It's true that we could kill Khan's flight crew outright, but I'm something of a groupie. *Baazigar* was a good movie. I'd hate to cause the man grief."

They stepped into the anteroom, and Mita swung a tiffin can into the back of Clapp's head. Her wig fell off as she fell to the ground. Erik prepared to attack Gaddis, but the big man threw a concussion grenade from his vest.

"Eyes and ears!" screamed Erik. Though they protected themselves from the light and noise, the blast knocked them to the floor. They scrambled to get up.

"Kill them!" screamed Clapp. They ran down the hall as Gaddis threw another flash-bang. Once more, they fell off balance and into walls. Ian ran into the small, dark room where Clapp had held him captive. He turned on the light. Erik and Mita stumbled in behind him.

Gaddis grinned. He had trapped them. The corridor would have been a better escape route. He let them wait in silence for a few moments, then tossed a grenade around the corner, into the room. The last thing he heard before it blew up inches from his head and killed him was the sound of it striking a cricket bat.

The blast knocked Erik unconscious. Ian, gripping the bat that he had retrieved from the corner of the room, was dizzy. Mita rubbed her eyes and her ears buzzed. The two ran to the antechamber as best they could. Clapp had taken the green-tagged tiffin cans and was nowhere to be seen. Only her wig remained.

They ran upstairs, out of the accounting office, through crowds that had scattered and panicked at the sound of the exploding grenades. Ian spied Clapp's bald head pushing the wheeled rack of tiffin dabbas to the exit. He clutched his cricket bat and ran for her with Mita behind him.

The police blew whistles. Ian closed the gap with the tiffin cart, swinging the bat and pushing people aside. A police officer dove at him. "Arrest her! She's trying to set off a bomb under the RBI with a remote control in her purse!" he screamed. "There's no time!" The officer did not understand. Ian neared Clapp and raised his bat to strike. A second police officer tackled him. Within seconds, six officers had piled atop Ian.

The security men rolled Ian onto his stomach, took his bat and handcuffed him from behind. From the ground, Ian watched Clapp push her tiffin cart into a van and drive away from the train station.

The officers stood Ian upright, but did not let him go. Ian leaned toward Mita.

"Tell Erik where I am when he wakes up. Find Clapp's wig."

"What about her wig?" Her ears continued to ring from the grenade.

"It's hair from Andhra Pradesh!" he screamed. She nodded, understanding. The officers pulled him toward a police car. "Mita! They're going to deport me for assault. I may not see you again! Thank you for everything!"

Mita Gavande rushed to him and kissed his cheek. He put his head next to hers and shouted things into her ear. She backed away and laughed as they locked eyes. "There's hope for you yet, Ian Racalmuto, be it sommelier or spy. Safe voyage, dear friend."

"I'll miss you!" said Ian. Tears filled his eyes as the police officers pulled them apart.

"You're crying," she shouted.

"The handcuffs hurt!" he said.

She rolled her eyes.

———

Vinita Clapp, under a large straw garden hat, drank white wine at a cafe table on the tarmac at Chhatrapati Shivaji International Airport. Several hundred yards away, over her shoulder, her henchmen finished fueling Shah Rukh Khan's private jet. The actor was on a shoot and unaware of her presence. The cart of tiffin cans was secure in the plane's cargo hold.

Clapp unfolded a pair of sunglasses and put them on. From her purse she extracted a remote control with a single button and extended a long wire antenna. She looked at her watch. At 15:00 hours, she pressed the button.

The airplane exploded. Heat bit her neck. Her straw hat blew onto the taxiway. The glass windows in the terminal shattered, and four hangars caught fire.

"The plan was a failure," said Clapp.

Clapp blinked. The blast had knocked her sunglasses crooked on her face. She lowered the antenna and replaced the detonator in her purse. She removed her phone.

"The plan was a failure," she told the voice on the other end. "Please assure that a clean-up crew attends to Gaddis."

At the end of the long corridor under the Reserve Bank of India, Mario, Deena, Cardiff, Erik, and Inspector Bharucha were opening tiffin cans, finding coins and artifacts stolen from across the city. Mita Gavande joined them. She explained that officers had arrested Ian for assault and attempted battery. Cardiff and Erik left to attend to the matter.

"How did her plan go so wrong?" asked Deena.

"Ian shouted into my ear before the officers took him away," said Mita. She pulled the red tag from the cart next to them. "Clapp appended colored labels to her carts. When we first arrived underground, Ian removed them for closer inspection. Clapp got the drop on him and held him at gunpoint. She told him to replace the tags, and he did. Only, he switched them. She didn't notice."

"Did he tell you anything else?"

Mita smiled. "He can tell you the rest some other time."

"How did Ian know where the green-tagged lunchboxes were going?" asked Bharucha.

"He didn't," laughed Mario. "He only knew Clapp wanted them. Details are sometimes secondary to desires."

"This isn't funny," said Deena, looking at Mario. "None of it is. Ian almost died. You think you're teaching him to be clever, but it isn't funny."

Mario responded only with a thin smile. Deena closed her eyes, held up her hands and turned away as she shook her head.

Erik and Ian sat beside one another on a jet that lifted from the runway toward Bangkok.

"I was hoping that the police at the train station would stop Clapp and find her with a cart full of explosives. They would have put her away for life," said Ian.

"You didn't get Clapp, but you did well," Erik replied. "Bharucha got a promotion."

"I can't enter India for ten years, Erik. Mom is pissed. The State Department may well send the two of you to the turkey farm. That isn't *doing pretty well.*" They listened to the engine noise and looked in opposite directions. "I'm glad Aadarsha's recovering well. It had to be rough finding her after the accident. How did you know what to do?"

"I didn't," said Erik. "There was nothing I could do. I didn't know the language, or who to call, or how to ask for help. So, I slumped down beside her like an asshole and hoped she didn't die until an ambulance arrived."

"Despair hurts," said Ian. "Sometimes heroes cry."

"Who said anything about crying?"

"We're made of the same cloth," said Ian.

Erik looked away and cracked his knuckles. "My neck hurt after the accident."

———

Mita Gavande entered a shop near Grant Road famous for selling high-end beauty products and hair. She produced Vinita Clapp's wig.

"This belonged to my late sister. It's from Andhra Pradesh."

The salesperson called a manager. Together, they admired its quality.

"I have no use for it," she continued. "Might I sell it back? She paid upward of two lakhs."

"We can give you one lakh," said the manager. "You're certain you want to part with it?"

Mita put on a white Ghandi cap. "It gets hot under my hat."

At twilight, an old caretaker rushed to the tower of silence on Malabar Hill. He had received a call about a broken lock. Tourists often asked to take photos inside the tower and some attempted entry without permission. He swung a torchlight around the excarnation site. Nobody was there. Nothing was out-of-place or missing. He prepared to leave but turned back.

There was a body he did not remember. It was upside-down. Vultures had picked the tissue away, but the bones were those of a short, fat man. There was a bullet fragment in his right hip.

The caretaker shrugged. After the wind, sun, and rain had their way, he would shove the skeleton into the ossuary pit where, with hundreds of others, it would crumble to dust.

END

CURSE OF THE EMERALD BUDDHA!

When 14-year-old Ian Racalmuto stepped from his taxi onto Khao San Road, he thought to a near-certainty he would melt under the penetrating sun. It was 10 AM. Bangkok was already alive with color, sound, and smell. Vivid neon signs advertised hostels and restaurants. Street vendors hawked clothing and souvenirs in a cacophony of tones, and the tantalizing scent of exotic spices wafted from food carts and outdoor grills. Try as he might, he failed to take in every detail of the bustling cityscape. Combined with the exhaustion of jet lag and the overwhelming urge to drink down an entire bottle of water at once, he could not form words and instead stood behind his sunglasses, immobile, breathing through his mouth.

"Welcome to Thailand," his grandfather, Mario, grinned. He brushed aside a sweaty strand of Ian's black hair and pushed up on his jaw, closing it with a finger. Mario glanced at Ian's brother, Erik, snapping photos on his phone.

To outside observers, they were a curious trio. Mario was an old black man with a mustache. Two generations later, Ian and Erik bore the olive complexion of their Italian mother, creating a striking contrast that seemed to defy the bounds of genetics. Erik, tall with a swimmer's build, was 10 years older than Ian and in the early days of a career in diplomacy. At 5-foot-three, Ian was short for his age, adding to the confusion. Hours ago, they landed on a flight from Mumbai, where a vacation had gone awry.

"If you see a vendor selling pineapple, let me know. The airplane food bound me," said Mario.

"I'm having the opposite issue," said Erik. "India is still having its way with me. I took an Imodium this morning."

"Imodium will stop you from sweating," said Ian. "Don't get heatstroke."

"Check it out," said Erik. He motioned toward a nearby vendor selling an assortment of vibrant masks under a sign that read *handmade*. Ian marveled at their intricate designs, his fingers tracing the wood. He picked two up and examined them. 350 *baht*. That's about ten bucks.

"What do you notice about the woodworking?" asked Mario from a distance.

"It's too precise," Ian said, at last. "And the antiquing is repeatable between samples."

"Fake," Ian and Erik mumbled in disappointed unison, replacing the masks on a table. Mario grinned.

They explored the city through the morning, finding themselves surrounded by ornate temples and golden spires piercing heaven. Ian could hardly believe the level of detail in the sculptures and murals he encountered. They filled the vacuum created by the disappointing souvenir masks. Only hours ago, he had barely considered Thailand as more than a spot on the map he'd likely never visit. Now, it was one of his favorite places in the world.

Mario pointed to a procession of saffron-robed figures walking through the crowd. Ian observed their serenity—a disposition so alien to him, he scarce believed it. How could this city evoke such emotion?

Mario led the way through the winding streets of Bangkok, his confident stride cutting a path for Ian and Erik to follow.

"Hey grandpop," asked Ian. "How do you know where you're going? Have you been here before?"

"Never," said Mario.

They passed through a plume of smoke from a charcoal grill where a vendor blackened succulent chicken skewers on the grate.

"That smells amazing," said Erik.

"*Swasdi khrab!*" Mario called out to the vendor, who responded with a warm smile and a nod. The Racalmutos stopped at the stall, where the aroma of grilled meats and vegetables mingled with the scent of exotic fruits.

"*Xea ki yang sxng loea phad thay hnung.*", Mario ordered, offering a few banknotes for skewers of chicken and a steaming plate of Pad Thai. "Some pineapple, too," he added.

Ian and Erik stared at each other.

Mario turned to them. "When you're here, you need to sample everything as often as you can. Otherwise, you'll go home thinking about all the things you missed."

"Back up," said Erik. "This is your first time here."

"How do you know Thai?" asked Ian. "I can practically hear all the little swirls and diacriticals of the script."

"I read the Frommer's book on the plane," said Mario, tapping his temple.

"Were you a spy in Indochina during the '70s?" asked Ian.

"I'm a suit salesman at Wanamakers," replied Mario, his enigmatic smile hinting at a secret he'd guarded since Erik was born, leaving the question of his past shrouded in intrigue.

After stopping for bottles of water, the trio stood before the majestic spires of Wat Arun, the Temple of Dawn. Throngs of people, both tourists and locals alike, milled around them, creating a quiet hum of voices, footsteps, and laughter. The sun cast a golden glow on the temple's sophisticated carvings, making it appear as though the structure itself was alive and breathing. Intricate porcelain tiles fit like shards of an enchanted puzzle.

"King Taksin built Wat Arun on the banks of the Chao Phraya River in the 1700s," said Mario, "when Siam was a distant dream."

Erik stared at Mario.

He cleared his throat. "Frommer's," he continued.

"I remember this place from school," said Ian. "The porcelain comes from broken Chinese dishes salvaged from a British shipwreck during the Ayutthaya Period."

Erik ignored them both and looked toward the river, distracted by a man chopping coconuts with a huge machete. Next to him was a woman selling pungent durian. The sculptures of fierce demons and benevolent deities stood guard, their eyes glaring in eternal vigilance.

Under a tent nearby, a woman wearing a straw hat sold small silver bells for 20 *baht*. Hundreds of them swung in rows beside her, attached to prayer cards, and jingled in the breeze. A large bronze bell hung over the unified display.

20 baht *for wishing bell*. Read a sign beside the woman. *Write your prayer on card and name on bell. Make wish. Hang up, then ring the big bell when finish.*

Erik read the instructions aloud, grammatical mistakes intact. He paid, took a prayer card, and wrote *a cold front, please*. He hung the silver bell with the card and rung the bronze bell overhead, pulling the clapper against the lip.

"Come true wish!" he said, sounding the bell repeatedly until the woman at the table stopped his hand and sent him away. His water was already warm, but he didn't care and gulped it.

Ian read the prayer cards. So many prayers. So many languages. The Chinese symbol for prosperity. A Canadian wishing for health. A note penned in a shaky hand, begging for relief of pain. What did he want? A few years ago, he might have written "a bicycle," but lately, as the realities of his life became clear, nothing material would suffice.

He scribbled a note on a prayer card, hoping the universe would listen and respond in kind. *Someone who can spin around on this rock with me.* He could feel his cheeks flush, and looked to his right, where Mario observed a wandering cat. Erik appeared from the left and plucked the card from his grasp before he could react.

"You're distracted, *fratellino*," said Erik.

"*Fottiti, stronzo!*" shouted Ian, swiping at the card but grabbing nothing but air. His face burned even hotter. "*Restituiscilo!*"

"Someone who can spin around on this rock with you!" Erik read aloud, laughing.

"Are we not good enough?" asked Mario.

"Is she going to be a blond or a brunette?" smiled Erik. "Tall?"

Ian hit Erik in the balls. "Short," he said. When his brother doubled over, Ian took the card back.

He attached the wish to the bell and hung it, then rung the big bell while Erik coughed and threatened to vomit.

"Your mom's expecting us at Chatuchak Market soon," said Mario.

"Can't keep Deena waiting," said Ian. He enjoyed calling his mom by her first name, because it irritated her.

The frigid air on the BTS Skytrain, a monorail connecting the city, offered a brief respite from humidity that now made Ian sweat through his clothing. He stopped by 7-Eleven for his third bottle of water in as many hours. "You both need to drink more," he cautioned Erik and Mario

"I had pineapple," said Mario.

"I don't need water," said Erik. "I don't want to spend all day peeing."

The market was a vast expanse of independent stalls, loosely organized by department. Many of the goods sold came from thrift stores in the United States that bundled and shipped them to the developing world. Merchants' voices filled the air, beckoning potential buyers to their packed shops: towers of exotic spices, rainbows of silken textiles, and an eclectic assortment of trinkets shimmering like buried treasure. Amidst the carnival of commerce, Deena Racalmuto navigated the foreign maze of with the practiced ease of a seasoned diplomat. Her trained eye flickered over the glittering display of accessory jewelry before her, pausing occasionally to admire an intricate piece or haggle over the price.

"Cardiff, what do you think of these earrings?" she called to her husband, holding up a pair of delicate silver hoops encrusted with tiny sapphires. "I could wear them to my firing this evening at the embassy."

"Hmm?" muttered Cardiff, his attention clearly elsewhere. A telephone call engrossed the milquetoast dentist, who nodded as he discussed a dental patient's surgery complications a world away from the vibrant chaos of the market. "Hold on," he told the patient. He turned to Deena. "They won't fire you," he said, returning to his call.

A distant blender hummed, and Erik excused himself to get a watermelon smoothie. "I'm not feeling so great," he said, woozy. Mario followed.

Ian looked at an array of used sneakers. In a Goodwill back home, he would have ignored them. Here, someone had arranged them on a display with such attention he could not resist them.

"One pair, five-hundred *baht*, two pair, eight seventy-five," called a voice.

Ian glanced up, immediately captivated by the speaker, whose English, though accented by Thai, was exceptional. He was a boy about his age. His skin, adorned with a few faint scars, carried a warm tan. He had chiseled features and sharp eyes with a mischievous glint. He swept his jet black hair to the side.

"What's your name?" asked the boy.

"Ian," said Ian, his voice hitching as it did when someone caught him off-guard.

"Ian, I have the perfect pair of shoes for you," said the boy. He ran across the stall and returned with a pair of old Adidas Sambas.

Ian, reluctant at first, tried them on. "What's your name?" he asked.

"Noc," said the boy. "Like the joke. Noc Noc."

"Who's there?" asked Ian.

"Noc!" said Noc, waving.

Ian laughed. "That's not quite how a knock-knock joke goes."

"It's not a knock-knock joke," said Noc. "It's a Noc-Noc joke. Do you want to see something cool?" he asked.

"I never turn down a chance to see something cool," said Ian.

Noc grabbed a piece of thin cardboard from a shoebox and folded it into a magnificent boat. He extended it to Ian. "For you."

"Thanks!" said Ian.

Noc withdrew the boat. "Free when you buy one pair of shoes for 500 *baht*, or two for 875."

Ian shook his head. "You own this shop?"

"It's my mom's. She has trouble working. A land-mine injured her leg in Laos when she was a girl, and she can't afford the surgery to fix it."

"It's nice of you," said Ian.

"I'd do anything for—"

Noc didn't finish. The air filled with a deafening blast, followed by an eruption of flames and smoke. The ground shook beneath their feet. Screams pierced the chaos, bringing the vibrant market to its knees.

"Deena?" Ian heard his father yell amidst the turmoil.

"Over there!" Noc shouted, pointing toward a tuk-tuk that barreled through the throngs of terrified people. Two men forced Deena onto the back seat, one gripping her arms and the other waving a knife. Her eyes met Ian's, and she pointed and screamed, "Ian! Grab my shopping bag! The bottle of vodka in it is too expensive to lose. My Walther is in there, and I don't have a secondary!"

"It's useless if it's out of reach, Deena," said Ian.

"Shut up!" shouted Deena, "and don't call me Deena!" The men pushed her down and drove off.

Ian grabbed her shopping bag, passed it off to his dad, and sprinted after the tuk-tuk. Noc darted towards a pair of Gojek dirt bikes parked nearby. He commandeered one, tossed a lime-green helmet to Ian, and mounted the other. Together, they tore through the crowded market in pursuit of the kidnappers.

"Stay close!" Noc yelled over the roar of the engines, weaving expertly through panicked shoppers and stalls ripped apart by the explosion. Ian's hands clenched tightly around the handles, knuckles white, as he sped after Noc, trying to keep up with the tuk-tuk.

Ian could hear Deena screaming. "Call the embassy! Tell them I'll be late to my firing!" He gritted his teeth and swerved to avoid a toppled fruit stand. Adrenaline pumped through his veins like liquid fire.

The tuk-tuk disappeared around a corner. Ian leaned into a sharp turn, narrowly dodging a group of shrieking market-goers, singed by debris. He could still feel the radiating heat of the blast.

Noc's engine sputtered. "Dammit!" he cried, slowing to a stop. Ian continued on, but emergency vehicles headed toward him blocked his path. Before the tuk-tuk dashed out of sight, however, he glimpsed a distinctive bumper sticker on the back. *8-Teen Massage*, it read.

Ian made his way back to Noc and skidded to a halt, his dirt bike kicking up dust and debris. Noc climbed on behind him, and they returned to Ian's family.

Mario leaned on a light pole, his leg bleeding and twisted. Cardiff had Diplomatic Security on the phone.

"The 8-Teen Massage Parlor!" Ian blurted out, fighting to catch his breath. "The Tuk Tuk had a bumper sticker for the 8-Teen Massage Parlor!"

Ian's hands clenched tightly around the handles, knuckles white, as he sped after Noc.

Cardiff relayed the information to the government officials on the other end of the line. Their response was far from reassuring. "They said to return to our hotel and wait," Cardiff reported, his voice tight with worry. "They'll handle it."

"Handle it?!" Ian exploded, fists clenching in frustration. "We can't just sit around while they have Mom! We've got a lead - we have to do something!" He looked back and forth between Cardiff and Mario. "Where's Erik?"

Mario pointed out a market stall selling T-shirts where Erik lay face-down on the floor. A shopkeeper had placed a fan at his head, and it blew his hair.

"The bomb?" asked Ian.

"The sun," said Mario.

"I told him to drink more water." He turned to Noc. "Do you know where the 8-Teen Massage Parlor is?"

"There are hundreds of such places in Bangkok," said Noc. "It would be impossible..."

"*Eccola qui*!" grinned Mario, looking at the address on his phone. "It's in Thonburi."

"We were just in Thonburi earlier," Ian said, "at Wat Arun. I don't know the streets, though." He turned to Noc. "Can you help?"

Noc nodded at the bike. "Get on."

"Nobody's going anywhere," Cardiff objected. "You're fourteen, Ian. You're not going to a Thai massage parlor. They're bastions of human trafficking. Your mother would have my head..."

Mario slipped a wad of cash into Ian's pocket. "Be careful," he whispered, as Cardiff carried on with explanations.

Ian mounted the dirt bike behind Noc.

"Are you even listening to me?" asked Cardiff.

The engine roared to life, drowning out the distant wails of sirens and chaos.

In the early evening light, Thonburi unveiled historical splendor against the backdrop of modernity. This district, once the capital of the Siamese kingdom, still retained remnants of its storied past. The temples took on a warm glow, and wooden stilt houses stood by the river, a testament to the area's timeless connection to the waterways.

The stench of cheap perfume and eucalyptus assaulted Ian's senses as he and Noc stepped into 8-Teen Massage. An obnoxious bell announced their arrival like an ill-omened gong, drawing the attention of a portly Thai woman of about 50 with tight-coiffed hair, painted eyebrows, and heels that echoed on the hard floor.

She unleashed a torrent of angry Thai words at Noc, her voice piercing. Ian's skin crawled with unease as he tried to decipher her agitation.

Noc's jaw clenched, but he held his ground.

"She doesn't want kids in her massage parlor?" asked Ian.

"Teens come here to lose their virginity every week," said Noc. "Mamasan doesn't want locals in her massage parlor."

"Mamasan?" asked Ian.

"That's her name," said Noc.

"Does she have a given name? A Thai name that doesn't dehumanize her for the Western gaze?"

Noc chattered back and forth with the woman. "She likes to be called Mamasan," he said. "She says she earned it."

"It just seems a little pejorative, is all," said Ian.

Mamasan raised an eyebrow.

"Americans find strange things important," said Noc.

Ian peeled several bills off the roll Mario gave him and handed them to Mamasan. "He stays with me," he said.

The squat woman grabbed the money and grunted, then ushered them to a seat outside the "Fishbowl"—a disturbing display window filled with scantily clad young women sitting on a carpeted dais, each numbered with a tag, staring vacantly and waiting for clients to select them for massages.

"Make selection, please," said Mamasan in broken English, gesturing towards the glass that separated Ian and Noc from the women. "What number?"

Ian's stomach churned. "I may be out of my depth," he muttered to Noc.

"Which one do you like?" Noc asked hesitantly, trying to maintain a casual tone. "That's how it works.

You pick a girl, they give us a massage... or other stuff."

Ian scanned the women, many from small villages, most looking for a path to prosperity. He searched for any reason to choose one over another. Huddled in a corner, out of place among her more confident workmates, was a bored woman with purple hair, tapping on her phone. A tattoo embellished her thigh—a serpent coiled around a dagger.

"What's that symbol?" asked Ian.

Noc squinted at the tattoo before a flicker of recognition crossed his features. "The Shadowlock syndicate," he said. "Art and antiquities thieves. They orchestrate high-profile art thefts and create forgeries-some for elite clients, others for lowly souvenir shops."

"Like the mask I saw today in the marketplace," said Ian.

"Tentacles everywhere," said Noc.

"Mom's a diplomat, and she was recently involved in investigations related to stolen artifacts. If she had come close to exposing this organization, it would make her a target," said Ian. "What's a member of Shadowlock doing in a massage window?"

"Let's find out," said Ian. He pointed at the woman with the tattoo and called her number in Thai.

Mamasan frowned and chattered.

"Perhaps another..." said Noc.

"No," Ian peeled another bill. "Her," he said.

"Darha," Mamasan said into a microphone, calling the tattooed woman from the fishbowl.

"*Khap khun khrab*," Ian said, thanking her in Thai. She stalked away, leaving them to follow the tattooed woman down a dimly lit hallway.

Ian's mind wandered, trying to figure out what was going through Noc's head. He knew a place buzzing with half-naked girls and the prospect of sex hanging in the air would electrify most guys. For Ian, it was different. These kinds of situations always felt like a maze of half-truths and awkward excuses. Everything fell apart between him and his friends when girls entered the picture. He could already picture Noc later, chattering about what he saw, leaving Ian with the tough choice of making up stories, skirting around the truth, or just clamming up. These moments always put cracks in the realness of his friendships.

"Hey Ian?" said Noc.

Ian's shoulders sunk.

Noc continued, "What should we have for dinner tonight? Pad Thai, maybe? I know a place with good Som Tum."

"I like papaya," Ian said, relieved.

"You buy," said Noc. "You never paid me for your shoes."

Upon reaching the massage room, the pungent scent of incense and the soft flicker of candlelight greeted them. Darha stood awkwardly by the massage table.

"You can remove your clothing," she said hesitantly, gesturing to the table. "What would you like today?"

Instead of undressing and lying down, however, both Ian and Noc perched on the edge.

"Information," said Ian.

She giggled. "You've spent a lot of money to waste my time."

"We're about to waste a lot more of it," said Ian. "Whoever you're waiting for in the fishbowl will not appreciate the delay."

Her smile faded, and she became silent. "You don't know what you're getting into."

"We'll hurry, but we need some details," said Noc.

"Are you cops?" she asked.

"I'm fourteen," said Ian. "I'm looking for my mommy. I don't care about your day-to-day business, or what your syndicate does. Has anyone hired your company for a big operation?"

Darha sighed. "A woman. She hired us to assist in an operation."

"Who?" asked Ian.

"I don't know her name. I've seen her three times. Each time, she has different hair."

"A different style?" asked Noc.

"No," said Darha. "Different hair. Wigs, I think. She also carried a small fan. I believe the Bangkok heat makes her sick."

"No," said Ian. "It's her climacteric. Her name is Vinita Clapp—a thief of art and antiquities I seem to keep running into. She's dangerous. What does she intend to steal?"

The door burst open before Darha could divulge further information, and Mamasan stormed in, enraged. She grabbed Darha by the arm and hurled her out of the room, screaming obscenities in Thai. With a final glare at Ian and Noc, Mamasan slammed the door shut, the sound of the lock clicking ominously into place.

"What happens next?" asked Noc.

"In my experience," said Ian, "Mamasan is going to ask her superiors what to do. They'll determine we know too much and attempt to kill us."

"So what do we do?" asked Noc.

Ian scoured the room. Aromatherapy diffuser. Soft towel. Clipboard on the back of the door. He removed it, disassembled it, and uncoiled a spring.

"Watch this," he said, and worked at the lock. "I like magic. I'm pretty good at picking pockets, making things disappear..." The lock clicked. "And picking locks."

Noc laughed, impressed.

They exited the room, finding themselves in a hallway now crowded with unfamiliar faces, all chattering anxiously about the potential misfortune that may befall the city if they remove "the object." At the other end of the hallway, Mamasan walked toward the massage room flanked by two burly men. Ian and Noc made for the front door before she could spot them in the crowd. The doorbell chimed its obnoxious tone, and they disappeared onto the busy street.

The sun dipped below the Bangkok skyline, casting a red glow over a night market coming to life. Shopkeepers stocked their racks; food vendors prepped for a busy night ahead. Noc navigated the crowd, leading Ian through a labyrinth of fragrant stalls offering an array of Thai street food. They passed by sausage skewers and steaming bowls of noodles, the intoxicating aroma of lemongrass, galangal, garlic, and Kaffir lime leaf filling the air.

"Try this," Noc said, ordering a sausage from a stall. The vendor put it in a clear plastic bag and drowned it in sweet chili sauce.

Ian took a bite, the juicy meat and containing depths and dimensions of flavor he had never thought possible. "If you order, I'll pay," he said. "I trust your judgment. It's amazing."

No sooner had Ian taken a food-filled paper bag from the vendor than Noc grabbed his wrist and pulled him onward.

"Where are we going?" asked Ian, between bites of satay, peanut sauce falling to the ground.

Noc flashed a grin, and lead him into a narrow alleyway at the edge of the market, where they found a rusted fire escape on an old building. Climbing the rickety metal stairs, they emerged onto the rooftop. The last of the day's sun reflected off the Chao Phraya river, its longboats and ferries continuing journeys north and south.

"Wow," breathed Ian.

"Beautiful, my city..." Noc said, leaning against the railing beside him.

They opened the bags of food and shared everything between them.

"I want to live here," Ian said.

"Why don't you?" asked Noc. "We could meet at night in the middle of the river, share good food, race boats... We could climb to the top of buildings and say, 'beautiful, *our* city.'"

Ian choked on his Pad See Eww, and swallowed hard.

Noc turned to face him. "My dad calls me childish. Tells me one day I'll want a family..."

"Yeah," said Ian.

"What do you think?" asked Noc.

"I'll win the boat race."

"That's not what I mean," Noc laughed. "Do you want a family? Do you want to work in government, like your mom?" he asked.

"I'm different," said Ian. "I want to be a sommelier. I like wine."

"Your nose isn't big enough," said Noc.

Ian shook his head and took another bite of food. "When we were leaving the massage parlor, everyone was talking about a misfortune that would befall the city. Does Bangkok have a protective talisman? A palladium? A work of art, a precious gem?"

"The Emerald Buddha at Wat Phao Kaew is sacred," said Noc. "It protects all Thailand, but it's on the grounds of the palace. It would be impossible to—"

"Nothing is impossible for Vinita Clapp," said Ian. "Something else bothers me. Remember how empty the hallway was when we arrived, and how crowded it was when we left?"

Noc snapped his fingers. "The doorbell. Why didn't we hear it?"

Ian looked out at the river, his hands now animated. "Point to the massage parlor."

Noc pointed west.

"And the Emerald Buddha?"

Noc traced a direct line east across the river to a point on the opposite shore.

Ian chewed on his lip, deep in thought. Noc smiled.

"What are you smiling about?" asked Ian.

"You talk with your hands when you get excited. It's funny."

Ian stuffed his hands in his pockets.

Without warning, the sky above the Chao Phraya river exploded with color. Ian ducked, memories of the marketplace bomb returning. Fireworks burst in vibrant hues of red, green, and gold, casting a kaleidoscopic glow over the water. The night market below erupted in cheers and laughter as people marveled at the display. Ian's heart raced with excitement, his worries forgotten.

"Wow," he breathed. "I've never seen fireworks this close."

"Fireworks are a big part of our celebrations," Noc explained, folding a paper boat from the discarded bag. "They chase away evil."

The colors continued to streak across the sky, and Noc turned toward Ian, his expression growing more serious. "Can I ask you something, Ian?"

"Sure," replied Ian.

"Of all the pretty girls in the fishbowl, which would you have picked for a massage?" Noc grinned.

Ian knew the question would manifest, and his cheeks grew warm. "Um," he stammered. "Well... I don't know. Why do you ask?" He shifted. "What about you?"

Noc shrugged and inched closer to Ian. "That's no answer. I'm not letting you off the hook. You had a good look at all of them."

"I did, but—"

Before Ian could continue, Noc closed the distance between them and pressed his lips against Ian's.

Ian grew dizzy and his breathing grew labored. His ears burned, and he blinked in surprise, unable to formulate a coherent thought.

"Wh-what was that for?" he stammered.

The colors continued to streak across the sky, and Noc turned toward Ian, his expression growing more serious. "Can I ask you something, Ian?"

Noc giggled. "I like you. I wanted to see if I could make you blush," he confessed with a sly grin. "I succeeded."

"Um," said Ian, trying to remain upright. He pointed to the paper boat in Noc's hand. "What's with the, uh, paper boats?"

"I love boats," said Noc. "My dad used to take me out on his, and taught me how to race."

"Is he still around?"

"I don't know. Maybe in Kuala Lumpur. I don't care." He handed the boat to Ian. "Until we can race real ones."

"Thanks." Ian struggled to focus and touched his mouth. He flapped his head. "Okay. Back to it. We need to figure out what's going on. My mom's life depends on it," he said.

Noc giggled.

"I think we should go back to the 8-Teen Massage Parlor," said Ian. "I'd like to have another look around."

"Shadowlock is dangerous," said Noc. "Maybe best to think this through longer?"

"The key to finding Deena lies with the syndicate, and all signs point to the 8-Teen. Don't worry. I'll keep us alive," said Ian.

"You're wrong," Noc replied. "We will keep each other alive. The bike is in the alley."

———

When they arrived, Mamasan was absent, replaced by a thin woman with a bright plastic smile. Ian walked past her, ignoring her greetings as though she were invisible, and swiped an incense stick on a small altar.

"Look at this," Ian said, nodding towards the smoke. It blew toward the fishbowl. He followed the trail to its source: a hidden door against the back wall.

Ian ran his fingers around the outline, looking for a switch or knob, but found only a hairpin on the floor. He clipped it to his shirt. Noc ran behind the front desk in the lobby and pressed a button underneath. With a quiet click, the door creaked open. "Found it!" he said.

A rush of damp, musty air greeted them—a blend of river water, mildew, and forgotten time. A serpentine passage stretched before them, hugged by rough-hewn stone walls and lit by dim, intermittent bulbs hanging from above. Overhead, rusted pipes dripped, adding an irregular rhythm to the echoes within.

To their left and right, storage alcoves carved into the walls emerged every so often like cathedral niches. Some, gated with bars, spoke of age and disuse, while others, open and dark, remained inscrutable.

They navigated the drab and narrow corridor, communicating through subtle gestures and whispers, ducking into alcoves to let workers pass. Ian admired Noc's ability to move through shadows, a skill honed from years spent navigating the bustling market crowds. Funny, he thought, how different upbringings could yield similar skills.

Noc nudged towards a series of open doors and gates. "Unlocked, already," he said.

Ian nodded. When at last they encountered a gate that remained secure, Noc's hands snatched Ian's hairpin from his shirt and went to work. With a deft motion, the lock sprung open, granting them access to the unknown depths ahead.

"Nice," Ian whispered, a small smile on his lips.

"I learned from a master," he said.

Ian reached around to the back of the gate and removed a skeleton key someone had left in the lock.

A large ruby embedded in the bow caught the faint light in the passageway. "Always check the backside of a gate first," he grinned.

Noc winced in embarrassment. Ian pocketed the key.

The damp, musty air clung to Ian's skin as they pressed on. The rumbling of water grew louder.

"We're under the river," said Noc.

"Who built this? And when? And why?" asked Ian.

Noc shrugged. "A king, a prince, a monk long ago... who knows? Thonburi was the original kingdom of Siam, so it makes sense to link the old city to the Grand Palace. What matters is where it goes."

They rounded a corner. Perfume filled their nostrils, and a familiar voice echoed from the stone walls.

"You don't find the name *Mamasan* a little pejorative?"

Ian's eyes grew wide. Deena!

"Americans find strange things important," Mamasan's voice replied. "Right now, you should not worry about my name. You should make peace with your deities. At midnight, once our task is complete, this tunnel will flood. I will not be here to share your fate."

"It's a pity," said Deena. "You need to wash off your shitty perfume. The fumes could kill me before I drown. They should give me hazard pay for having to endure it."

Ian giggled. "Keep talking, Deena," he whispered, following the sound of her voice.

"The embassy is supposed to be firing me right now," Deena continued. "My son nearly blew up India. Because of this little charade, I'm going to be late. They'll probably have to fire me twice."

"Will you shut up?" asked Mamasan. "You talk, talk, talk."

"How did you end up assigned to me, Mamasan?" Deena continued. "This isn't your normal gig. Were they short on help? Did someone call in sick? Did you draw a tiny lot? You're truly incompetent as a captor."

Ian and Noc at last located a small chamber off the main passage, and spied Deena's shadow. She sat in a chair, struggling against ropes.

"Ian ties better knots in his shoelaces," Deena said.

Mamasan tugged the ropes tighter. Her patience wore thin, her eyes narrowing as she clenched her fists. Ian shared a glance with Noc, silently communicating their need for a plan. Noc spotted a loose stone near the chamber wall. He gestured towards it before miming an exaggerated throw.

"Perfect," Ian said, impressed by Noc's quick thinking. "I'll toss the rock against the wall and distract her."

"Can you throw?" asked Noc.

"Like Dock Ellis on LSD," Ian whispered. He gathered the rock and pitched it as hard as he could toward the back wall. It sailed nowhere near his target, and instead struck Mamasan in the back of the head, knocking her out cold.

Noc ran forward and untied Deena. Ian gave her a tremendous hug.

"Thanks," Deena said, rubbing her wrists. They lifted Mamasan into the chair, binding and gagging her. "Where does this tunnel lead?" she asked.

Ian pointed behind him. "The massage parlor is that way. I don't know what's ahead."

"Better find out," Deena urged. "I'll be fine from here. Stay together."

Ian and Noc nodded to each other and continued their journey down the passageway. After a few hundred yards, the air freshened. They emerged at Wat Phra Kaew, set within the grandeur of the Grand Palace grounds.

Inside the temple chamber, intricate gold-leaf patterns covered the walls and caught the dim light. The Emerald Buddha sat atop a golden pedestal, its serene expression a stark contrast to the chaos of the past five hours. The Buddha's manageable size and low weight hinted at the ease with which Clapp could transport it through the tunnel. It wore a makuta and enameled gold, emanating tranquility and warmth.

"They change the Buddha's clothes thrice yearly, with the seasons," said Noc.

"I wonder who purchases the objects Clapp sells?" asked Ian.

"This one I intend to put on my lanai near my outdoor fireplace," said a raspy female voice.

The cold metal of a gun barrel pressed against Ian's back. "Hello, boys."

Ian's eyes found Noc. Mamasan emerged from the shadows, an ice bag against her head, and held him at gunpoint, too.

"Hey Noc?" asked Ian, raising his hands in surrender. "I can't see who's shoving a gun in my back. Is she wearing a wig?"

Noc shook his head in the negative.

"Is she bald?" he asked.

Noc shook his head in the affirmative. A bead of sweat trickled down Ian's temple.

"Does she look menopausal?"

"Shut up!" hissed the woman behind him.

"Hello, Vinita," said Ian.

"Ian Racalmuto," said Vinita Clapp. "How you end up wherever my business takes me is beyond my comprehension."

"How *you* end up everywhere *I* am ruins my vacations," said Ian.

Clapp and Mamasan nudged the two boys forward with their weapons. "Back in the passageway, both of you," Clapp ordered. Her bald head gleamed menacingly under the evening light. Mamasan's lips twisted into a cruel smile.

"Twice you have ruined my operations this year," said Vinita. "It won't happen again. At midnight, I'll steal the Emerald Buddha from the temple, flood the tunnel you've capably discovered, and leave you both in watery graves."

"Already heard that part," Ian said. "Mamasan was flapping her gums to my mom about all of this before she escaped."

Vinita's eyes narrowed. Her face became crimson. She turned to Mamasan, who cringed. "You told them?"

"Yes, but—"

"And let them tie you to a chair while their mother escaped?"

"Ms. Clapp, I—"

"It was my plot to reveal," she said.

"I'm sorry…" said Mamasan.

"Nincompoop," Clapp muttered.

Mamasan's stuttered.

Clapp continued, "It's of no consequence. By the time your mother convinces Thai police of anything, the deed will be done." She handed Mamasan a cellular phone—a silver brick with an orange antenna. "This has only one pre-programmed number, which you will find in the menu. Text the code, 7-3-8-9, at midnight, but not before." Clapp smirked at Ian, adding, "Mamasan rigged dynamite throughout the passage."

Ian's heart pounded in his chest. He had been in near-death situations before, but this was different. He thought of Noc's mom, managing her store alone with her injured leg, grieving the death of her only boy. "What do you want, Vinita?" said Ian. "To be left alone to your devices? I can do that."

"There's nothing you can give me I don't already have," said Clapp. She turned her attention to Noc, her eyes cold as ice. "And there's no way you're saving him."

Mamasan took Noc deep into the tunnel. He hesitated for a moment, his gaze lingering on Ian before she forced him away.

Clapp moved Ian into an alcove and locked him behind an iron gate. Overhead, a monstrous fan turned, its blades casting sinister shadows that flickered across the damp walls. Cold air cut through his skin, raising goosebumps.

"This is the second time your operations have involved a subterranean passageway," said Ian. "Were they offering you a discount for two?"

"It isn't easy to find subterranean contractors," said Clapp, "so as long as you have them for one job, you might as well use them for everything. They're fixing the bathroom in my basement at home, too. Right now, if there's a heavy rain, the toilet overflows. Anyway... you have your choice: you can drown when the tunnel floods, or take your chance escaping through the fan shaft." She pressed a button, and the blades turned faster. "Or maybe the rising water will carry you into the blades..." she muttered to herself. "Either way, you'll die. Goodbye, Ian." She spun on her heel.

"Like my mom always says," Ian started, "no good about—" Clapp vanished, and he did not finish. He swallowed hard and studied the lock. He moved his hand to the back, but found no key.

He searched his pockets. Noc had taken his bobby pin, but what about the ruby key he pocketed earlier? He inserted it in the lock and turned it with a satisfying click. The gate swung open with a rusty groan, and he stepped into the treacherous underground passageway.

"No way," he laughed. He made his way toward the massage parlor, listening for voices, hiding from workers, and peering into dark voids. A few minutes before ten, a familiar scent filled his nose: Mamasan's cheap perfume.

"Noc, Noc!" came a voice behind him.

"Who's there?" asked Ian, spinning around.

"Noc!" said Noc, sitting bored behind an iron gate in an alcove similar to the one in which Clapp jailed Ian. His expression quickly relaxed. "I thought you were gone!" Noc continued.

"Not without you," said Ian.

"I tried to pick the lock, but failed," said Noc. "I'm lousy at this game."

"No you aren't," said Ian. "You can't pick *every* lock."

"How did you escape?" asked Noc. Ian held up the ruby key. He moved to free Noc, but the key didn't work.

The sharp clack of Mamasan's heels echoed through the labyrinth's twisted passageways.

"I'm going to let Mamasan unlock it for us," said Ian. "Don't go anywhere." He disappeared into the darkness.

Mamasan held her phone to her ear and rubbed the sore spot on her head. A few minutes ago, her sister had called. "In all my years..." she said in Thai as she walked. "I have a business to run, and she has me playing dungeon keeper with children. What? I can't hear you. I'm under the river while she plays tomb raider. What? How the hell should I know?"

An unexpected sound sharpened her focus—a sudden, ill-timed sneeze, startlingly close. Her hand flew to her phone, her thumb activating the flashlight in one motion. The beam sliced through the blackness, revealing Ian, crouched in a cramped nook, his eyes wide.

He lunged from the shadows, his movements a blur. They collided, a tangle of limbs. Then, with a swift, viper-like motion, Mamasan drew her gun. She thrust the barrel against Ian's forehead, and herded him, with a menacing calm, toward the alcove where Noc stood behind the gate.

Mamasan withdrew a key from her pocket and unlocked it. It creaked open, its hinges screeching in protest. Ian stumbled into the alcove, shooting Noc a fleeting glance. A silent plan passed between them.

Like a coiled spring unleashed, the boys jumped into action. They thrust the heavy iron gate forward with a surge of adrenaline-fueled strength. It smashed against Mamasan's wrist with brutal force. A piercing scream tore from her lips, the sound raw and shocking in the confined space. Her gun, caught in the chaos, clattered away.

The alcove erupted into a maelstrom of desperation and fury. Ian and Noc grappled with Mamasan, their movements frantic, each trying to gain the upper hand.

Noc and Ian shoved Mamasan against the cold, damp wall of the alcove, her breaths ragged gasps. They scrambled out, and in a last burst of effort, slammed the gate shut. A resounding clang reverberated through the passageway. Noc's hand, shaking with exertion and relief, twisted the key in the lock.

Ian stuck the key in his pocket beside the one with the ruby bow. "I'll have a collection by the time we finish," he said.

Stepping back, the boys panted, their bodies battered and bruised but alive with the rush of their narrow escape. They watched Mamasan's figure, caged and defeated, become a silhouette of rage, her shouts of fury diminishing into the corridor's shadows.

When Ian and Noc emerged from the underground passageway into the fishbowl at the massage parlor, Vinita was nowhere to be found

"Damn it!" Ian hissed through gritted teeth. "Where could she be?"

"She's headed to the river." It was Darha. "She's using a dragon boat as a command center."

"Why should I believe you?" asked Ian

"Because she left without paying me," said Darha.

———

The river lived and breathed, and snaked its way through Bangkok. In its basins arose the earliest civilizations of Southeast Asia. Its waters were a deep black at night. The gentle lapping of the waves against the shore hypnotized passers-by, and belied swift currents and dangerous traffic.

"This way!" said Noc, sprinting to a nearby dragon boat, its vibrant colors barely visible.

Ian searched the water and found a similar boat, already launched. In it sat a woman, the moon reflecting from her head. "There she is!" he shouted. He peered at the outboard motor and wavered. The midsection of the engine stretched out like the tail of a sea creature, the propeller mounted directly on the driveshaft. "Do you know how to—"

Noc pushed him out of the way and started the engine.

"I'm no good with lock-and-key subterfuge," he said, "but I can drive a dragon boat. You have to be careful. Crank the power plant too fast, and we'll end up in the drink."

He gripped the throttle and pursued Clapp.

Vinita's boat picked up speed, weaving through the nighttime river traffic.

A bulky cargo boat loomed ahead, nearly invisible in the darkness. Noc's heart raced. He steered the dragon boat to the right, narrowly avoiding a disastrous collision.

"Can you pilot close to the shore?" Ian asked, his voice thick with urgency. "There's something I want to grab."

Noc steered close to land, never losing sight of Vinita's boat. The sounds of bustling night markets and laughter-filled bars floated across the water.

They passed within inches of a pier, and Ian snatched a discarded cargo net.

"Now," said Ian, "Let's get her!"

Noc throttled up, but a water taxi pulled in front of them. Noc maneuvered around it with precision, a rush of air as their hulls passed close. A boatswain on the taxi whistled in anger.

Vinita glanced back, spotting their pursuit. Her face hardened, and she pushed her boat's throttle, the engine roaring. The gap between them widened, but Noc remained unshaken.

A brightly lit cruise ship cut across their path. Noc steered left, the boat's motor straining as they skirted the cruiser's stern. Its wake sent them rocking.

"Stay on her!" Ian shouted against the wind and engine's roar. Noc, his hands steady on the throttle, nodded. He knew the Chao Phraya, its currents and secrets, better than anyone.

Clapp failed to anticipate a swift current. Her boat wobbled and lost momentum. Seizing the opportunity, Noc closed the gap.

Ian leaned out, the boat's prow nearly touching the churn of Vinita's propeller. His eyes met Clapp's for a moment—a mix of determination and realization. He extended his hand, the cargo net ready, and tossed it into her prop.

The net ensnared her engine. Her eyes widened with shock before narrowing into a venomous glare as her boat slowed amid the gurgling sound of the motor choking.

"Got her!" Ian exclaimed, a triumphant grin spreading across his face. "Let's head to shore," said Ian. "She's not going anywhere. I'll make some calls."

Something was out-of-place. Noc directed the boat alongside Clapp's.

"To shore!" Ian repeated. It didn't matter. They were now mere feet from Clapp. She withdrew a gun and leveled it at them.

"How much gas do we have, Noc?" she asked.

Ian looked at Noc, the color draining from his face.

"Enough," said Noc.

Clapp waved the gun, pointing Ian onto her disabled boat. They traded places, and she kicked the two boats apart.

"It was a nice effort," said Clapp, "but you underestimate the complexity of my network." She turned to Noc. "Mamasan?"

Noc pointed his thumb at Ian. "I picked his pocket," he said, "and left the key with her."

Ian reached into his pocket and found only lint. "Noc?" his voice cracked, heavy with disbelief.

"I'm sorry," Noc said, his voice tinged with desperation. "My mom... I'd do anything for her... you understand how that is."

"My mom would amputate her leg before allowing me to do what you're doing now," said Ian. "Turning to Clapp won't save her. Clapp will hang you out to dry. She won't pay you. Not you, not your mom, not anybody."

Noc's eyes flickered with a mixture of hope and naivety. "She'll get the surgery she needs. She won't have to work at the market selling old shoes, and neither will I."

Ian's voice trembled. "I get it, Noc. Life tosses us some shit. Sometimes there are no straightforward answers. But you can't pick every lock. I'd sell shoes with you if we could hang out together like on the rooftop."

"Together?" asked Clapp.

Noc stuck his tongue in his cheek. "I did what I had to do," he said.

Clapp grinned. "I should pay you double."

The river had become a whirlpool to Ian, each revelation dragging him deeper into a cold, unfathomable abyss. "You'll be lucky if she doesn't pay you in lead when she finishes," he said. "Your grand illusion of easy wealth? It's a shimmering dream, gone by dawn like every other."

"The only thing that will be gone at dawn is the Emerald Buddha," said Clapp. She turned to Noc. "You'll have your money."

Ian returned his hand to his pocket, his expression somber. "No, Noc, you won't."

"What do you know?" asked Noc.

"You picked my pocket. *I* picked Mamasan's."

He held up Mamasan's silver phone, its orange antenna a stark contrast in the moonlight.

"Last I checked," Ian continued, "It was still over an hour before midnight." He keyed in a sequence, his voice barely above a whisper. "Seven. Three. Eight. Nine."

"NO!" Clapp's shriek cut through the night. She reached in her pocket for her gun.

"Noc Noc," said Ian. His thumb struck one last button.

A low rumble crescendoed. A massive water column erupted into the sky, spanning the two shores downstream. The hidden tunnel beneath the river exploded, its purpose unfulfilled. A shockwave lifted their boats, tossing Noc and Clapp toward the land, and Ian further from shore.

"You fool!" cried Clapp. "You just lost *my* money and *your* life!" She pointed her gun toward Ian and retracted the hammer. "By the time they find you adrift, your blood will have drained from the hole in your head into the bilge."

"Pull it," said Ian, looking at Noc. "I don't give a shit."

Noc's eyes welled with tears. He gripped the boat's throttle and gave it a sharp twist. Clapp's boat lurched forward, and she lost balance. Her gun discharged into the sky and fell into the water. Before she could stand again, the boat was underway toward the city.

———

Hours passed, and night turned into early morning. The river came to life. Ian Racamuto barely noticed, his head buried between knees hugged to his chest.

An outboard motor grew loud. "This is all your fault," said Deena. "Who gives a fourteen-year-old boy money to go to a Thai massage parlor? It's unconscionable."

"You went there, too," said Mario.

"I was a hostage!" shouted Deena. "I had no option!"

"There he is!" said Mario.

"This doesn't look good," said Mario.

They pulled their boat next to Ian's. Ian's head remained down.

"This doesn't look good," said Mario.

"Ian?" asked Deena. "What's wrong? What happened?"

"Where's your friend?" asked Mario.

Ian lifted his chin, his eyes red and swollen. "I should have known," he said. "He knew where the switch to the door in the fishbowl was. He knew where to find a dragonboat. *He* set off the bomb in the market. He pretended he—" He stopped and turned away and sniffed hard. "Why didn't I question any of it? Where was my head? Why didn't I see it? Why did I believe it?"

"Sometimes we don't have all the facts," said Mario. "We muddle along and do the best we can until we do."

"The Buddha's still in its rightful place," said Deena. "You did good."

Ian stared out at the river, still a dark ribbon in the dim light of dawn. "Yeah, the Buddha's safe," he uttered. "And today, worshipers will visit like nothing happened and share their hopes and dreams and wishes. Kinda funny, isn't it? Everyone trusts a piece of stone more than they trust real people. I get why. I'm a little envious. The Buddha just sits there, not having to deal with getting stabbed in the back or let down. Must be nice, not having to feel any of that."

Mario sighed. "Let's get out of here, kid."

Ian, Mario, and Erik walked around Wat Arun. Ian wanted to see it one last time before leaving Bangkok.

"How long before we have to leave for Suvarnabhumi?" asked Erik.

"Five minutes," said Mario, "if we want to make our flight."

Ian returned to the wishing bell and searched through the prayer cards. After a few minutes, he found his. He removed it and ripped it into shreds, letting the confetti blow toward the river.

"We can go?" asked Erik.

Ian turned to leave, but something caught his eye. A prayer card folded into a paper boat. He unfolded it.

Among the many wishes that drift in the wind, mine is that you find someone as true as your heart. I'm sorry.

Ian let his hand, clutching the note, fall to his side.

"We need to go," said Erik.

"Coming," said Ian. They walked toward a dock where a water taxi would collect them. On the path, flies circled a metal drum filled with spent coconut husks and rotting, slimy durian peels. Mario recoiled at the stench.

Ian crumped the note and stuffed it into the putrid effluvium.

END

NO GOOD ABOUT GOODBYE
A Novel by CT Liotta

A 2022 IndieBRAG medallion recipient

Ian Racalmuto can handle assassins, bombs and bullets... but harboring a crush on his best friend? Stopping world war is easier.

15-year-old Ian Racalmuto's life is in ruins after an embassy raid in Algiers. His mother, a vodka-drunk spy, is dead. His brother, a diplomat, has vanished. And, he's lost a cremation urn containing a smartphone that could destroy the world.

Forced to live with his cantankerous grandfather in Philadelphia, Ian has seven days to find his brother and secure the phone—all while adjusting to life in a troubled urban school and dodging assassins sent to kill him.

Ian finds an ally in William Xiang, an undocumented immigrant grappling with poverty, a strict family, and abusive classmates. They make a formidable team, but when Ian's feelings toward Will grow, bombs, bullets and crazed bounty hunters don't hold a candle to his fear of his friend finding out. Will it wreck their relationship, roll up their mission, and derail a heist they've planned at the State Department?

Like a dime store pulp adventure of the past, *No Good About Goodbye* is an incautious, funny, coming-of-age tale for mature teens and adult readers.

Scan the QR Code above to purchase!

Rot Gut Pulp: *Entertainment, not Genius.* ™

CT Liotta was born and raised in West Virginia before moving to Ohio for college, where he majored in Biology. He now uses Philadelphia as his base of operations. You can find him backpacking all over the world. For wesbsite, newsletter, and information about all books and writing, visit:

https://www.ctliotta.com

or scan the QR code above.